Tales of Merlin, Arthur, and the Magic Arts

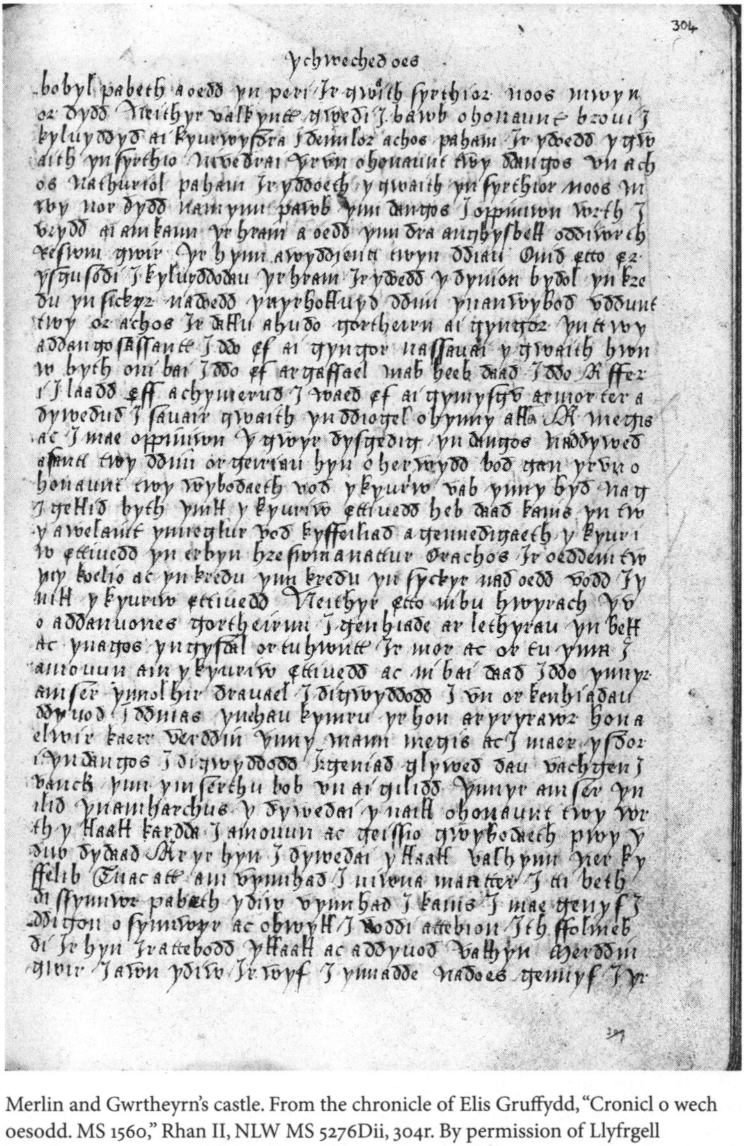

Merlin and Gwrtheyrn's castle. From the chronicle of Elis Gruffydd, "Cronicl o wech oesodd. MS 1560," Rhan II, NLW MS 5276Dii, 304r. By permission of Llyfrgell Genedlaethol Cymru / The National Library of Wales.

Tales of Merlin, Arthur, and the Magic Arts

From the Welsh Chronicle of the Six Ages of the World

Elis Gruffydd

Introduction by Jerry Hunter
Translations by Patrick K. Ford

UNIVERSITY OF CALIFORNIA PRESS

University of California Press
Oakland, California

Library of Congress Cataloging-in-Publication Data
Gruffydd, Elis, approximately 1490–approximately 1552, author. |
Ford, Patrick K., translator. | Hunter, Jerry—writer of introduction.
Title: Tales of Merlin, Arthur, and the magic arts : from the Welsh Chronicle of the six ages of the world / Elis Gruffydd ; introduction by Jerry Hunter ; translations by Patrick K. Ford.
Other titles: Cronicl o wech oesoedd. Selections. English
Description: [Oakland, California] : [University of California Press], [2023] | Includes bibliographical references.
Identifiers: LCCN 2022026767 (print) | LCCN 2022026768 (ebook) |
ISBN 9780520390256 (paperback) | ISBN 9780520390263 (ebook)
Subjects: LCSH: Tales—Wales. | Tales, Medieval—History and criticism.
Classification: LCC GR150 .G78 2023 (print) | LCC GR150 (ebook) |
DDC 808.8/0358207—dc23/eng/20220624
LC record available at https://lccn.loc.gov/2022026767
LC ebook record available at https://lccn.loc.gov/2022026768

Manufactured in the United States of America

28 27 26 25 24 23
10 9 8 7 6 5 4 3 2 1

Merlin/Taliesin Speaks

Myui a vum ymlygiawd
yngwlad y Drindawd
a nyui a vum ddysgogawd
i'r holl uyddygawd
a myui a vyddaf hyd dydd brawd
ar wyneb daiarawd
Ac ni widdis beth yw vy nghnawd
Ai kig ai pisgawd . . .
Shihannes ddewin
a'm gelwis J Merddin,
Bellach poob preenin
a'm geilw J Taliesin

I was revealed
in the land of the Trinity
and I was moved about
throughout Christendom [or: the world]
and I will endure till Judgment Day
upon the face of the earth
and no one knows whether my flesh
is meat or fish . . .
John the Divine
called me Merlin
now every king
calls me Taliesin

CONTENTS

Introduction

Elis Gruffydd and His Chronicle

This book is about the legendary figures of Merlin and Arthur as depicted in the many original Welsh folktales left out of the widespread accounts of their exploits in English, Latin, and French through which most people know these stories today. But it is also about the survival of the magical arts from antiquity to the Renaissance and the broader cultural world of the Welsh, who were finally conquered and colonized by the Normans and the English during the medieval period but whose language and traditions were never extinguished.

The stories translated here have been culled from a single source, the enormous, sixteenth-century chronicle of Elis Gruffydd, written in his native Welsh. Its more than two thousand pages tell the history of the world from the Creation to the reign of Henry VIII, the author's contemporary, in exhaustive detail, including feats of the leading figures in histories of Europe. Much of Elis's masterpiece, however, can be tedious and tiresome for those not interested in the succession of popes or political maneuverings of princes. But tucked away among such political, military, and historical details are wonderful stories from the popular culture of the times that reflect the beliefs and fears of the people, commoners and elites alike, among whom such stories and beliefs circulated. This near-forgotten voice from the sixteenth century offers a treasure-house of sustained exploration of the widespread belief in the powers of magic, necromancy, prophecy, and related mystical arts, with Merlin and Arthur playing prominent roles.

Importantly, this book is also about the survival and adaptation of tradition, as it demonstrates how medieval Welsh thinking about Arthur and his court—a body of legends indigenous to Wales and the Britons who ruled the island before the arrival of the Romans and later the Anglo-Saxons—continued into the sixteenth century, often in ways that combined influences from other countries with the native stories about these most Welsh of heroes.

Elis used a dizzying combination of sources in a variety of languages, not only written works but also folklore, rumor, and hearsay. Crucially, these include not just the French and Anglo-Saxon compilations that today's readers know best but also the many Welsh folktales never recorded in these foreign collections. Indeed, the versions of the tales that modern readers know all come from nonnative accounts written in foreign languages long after the stories originally circulated—like reading about the Homeric heroes in a Turkish retelling. When you're reading Arthurian Romances, you're reading the twelfth-century collection of a Frenchman, Chrétien de Troyes; if you read Geoffrey of Monmouth's history of the kings of Britain, you're reading the work of a British cleric writing in Latin. The English *Le morte d'Arthur* was written by Thomas Mallory in the fifteenth century. Although Elis was writing about the legends and history of Britain from the perspective of a century later, as a Welsh speaker he was privy to long-standing native oral traditions and folktales and to Welsh-language texts no longer extant today.

The general shape of the stories of the births of Merlin and Arthur and their subsequent careers may be broadly familiar to readers, but the treatment of the material here is uniquely Welsh, with many of the details found nowhere else. While Merlin and Arthur are no doubt the most recognizable, there are many other legendary and historical figures of antiquity and medieval Romance who populate these pages. Taken as a whole, these stories have a very high entertainment value and provide a window onto a world that suffered through numerous plagues and near-constant political strife. It was a world that men of the "arts" attempted to tame through prophecy, necromancy, sorcery, astrology, and other forms of magic. This book offers a unique and much-needed perspective on these remarkable characters and the world of medieval Wales.

THE CHRONICLER AND HIS MASTERPIECE

Elis Gruffydd was born in Flintshire in north Wales around 1490; his home was at Gronant Uchaf in the parish of Llanasa (or Llanasaph), less than a mile from the Pantyllongdy home of Tomas fab Tomas fab Gruffudd Fychan, apparently a close relative. The historian Prys Morgan has described Elis as a member of the poorer branch of a minor-gentry family. He was intensely literate in his native language, was able to read several other languages, and surely had some kind of education before leaving Wales. Morgan also suggested that Elis might have had some bardic instruction in his early years.[1] As will be seen below, Elis certainly recorded a considerable amount of other people's poetry in manuscript, including strict-meter bardic compositions. As wealthier branches of his extended family maintained houses of some stature, it is possible that he had some contact with the peripatetic poets of north Wales during his early life, perhaps hearing bardic works performed there or in the houses of neighbors. However, given the fact that Elis was by no means averse to writing about himself and describing his own accomplishments, one would expect to find examples of his own poetry in his manuscripts, had he written any.[2] Although Ceridwen Lloyd-Morgan's hypothesis that Elis was instructed by one or more of the monks from the Cistercian Valle Crucis Abbey during his youth is ultimately unprovable, it is easier to accept than imaging him as a bardic pupil who never recorded any of his own poetry. All that can be said with certainty is that Elis was extremely literate and thus educated in some manner, and that he definitely did not attend a university.[3]

Elis's chronicle of the six ages of the world is one of the longest works ever composed in the Welsh language. It consists of more than

1. Prys Morgan, "Elis Gruffydd of Gronant—Tudor Chronicler Extraordinary," *Flintshire Historical Society Publications* 25 (1971): 11. The spellings .-*udd* and -*ydd* both occur in Elis Gruffydd's written name, the two vowel sounds in unstressed syllables having coalesced by the late medieval period.

2. For example, in recording information about the defenses of Calais, Elis notes that he himself was responsible for maintaining one of the outer bulwarks (Mostyn 158, 583r–v; see n. 4 below).

3. Ceridwen Lloyd-Morgan, "Elis Gruffydd a Thraddodiad Cymraeg Calais a Chlwyd," *Cof Cenedl* 11 (1996): 31-58.

2,400 large manuscript pages and takes as its subject the entire history of the world, from the beginning of humanity as described in the Christian Bible up to the year 1552.[4] It draws upon a dizzying collection of sources, written in different languages—Welsh, English and French, Latin, and possibly Flemish—and ranging from manuscripts and printed books to oral history, rumor, and folktale. Elis's world history includes events in *y dwyrain,* "the east," and the "discovery" of America. However, a combination of factors—including his personal interests, the way in which he imagined his readership, and the sources available to him—ensured that the work focuses increasingly on Britain (seen first as the realm of *yr Hen Frytaniaid,* or "the Ancient Britons") and then on England, Wales, and France.[5] Patrick K. Ford, the translator of the stories in this book, has provided a means for readers to familiarize themselves with these aspects of the chronicle, for he includes a narrative here titled "The Origins of Britain" and stories about various monarchs of Wales, England, and France, as well as ones involving the Welsh princes.

Elis wrote this great work while serving as a professional soldier in Calais, the English monarchy's last foothold in France. In many ways his work and what we know of him suggest that his life was paradoxically both emblematic of many Welsh experiences during the Tudor period and totally unique. Although the medieval bardic tradition continued throughout the sixteenth century, a very different kind of Welsh literati were challenging the bards' time-honored cultural hegemony before the end of Elis's life. In that tradition, professional poets under-

4. The chronicle is in two volumes, now labeled NLW MS 5276D and NLW MS 3054D (the latter also called Mostyn 158, in reference to an earlier manuscript collection to which it belonged), both in the manuscript collection of the National Library of Wales and each divided into two parts. Excellent digital images of the entire work are available thanks to the NLW: see https://www.library.wales/discover/digital-gallery/manuscripts/early-modern-period/elis-gruffudds-chronicle.

5. Much of the following discussion draws upon my earlier works *Soffestri'r Saeson[:] Hanesyddiaeth a Hunaniaeth yn Oes y Tuduriaid* (Cardiff: Gwasg Prifysgol Cymru, 2000) and "The Chronicle of Elis Gruffydd" (PhD diss., Harvard University, 1995). For more information about the wider literary contexts discussed here, see A.O.H. Jarman et al., eds., *A Guide to Welsh Literature* (Cardiff: University of Wales Press, 1992–98); Geraint Evans and Helen Fulton, eds., *The Cambridge History of Welsh Literature* (Cambridge: Cambridge University Press, 2019); Damian Walford Davies, ed., *The Oxford Literary History of Wales,* vol. 1 (Oxford: Oxford University Press, forthcoming).

went years of training before graduating into the upper echelons of the bardic order and being licensed to compose and perform strict-meter praise poetry for *uchelwyr*, members of the Welsh gentry. Bards often served as manuscript copyists as well and were thus guardians and transmitters of traditional Welsh letters and learning by multiple means. Now, however, university-educated humanists were an increasing cultural force, sometimes openly criticizing the traditional bards and debating ways in which the Welsh language and its literature could be developed and enriched, as well as ensuring the publication of the first Welsh books, in the 1540s. Elis did not attend university and so did not receive formal exposure to the *studia humanitatis* curriculum, and thus he cannot be described as a humanist in the strict sense. However, his work displays a commitment to what can be described more loosely as a humanist educational agenda.[6] By the same token, he was not a bard, although he was certainly exposed to a great deal of bardic learning and compositions, as will be discussed below. Elis created the longest work of Welsh-language literature produced up to that point, yet he belonged to no established Welsh literary milieu; while this might be seen as paradoxical, his lack of formal affiliation might also help explain the unique nature of his literary contribution.

Given the nature of the native and domestic literary tradition into which Elis was born, it is noteworthy that his chronicle was composed in Calais by a Welshman who lived most of his life beyond the borders of the land of his birth. The phrase *self-imposed exile* is perhaps not accurate, given the fact that Elis clearly embraced the career that kept him first campaigning on the continent, then living and working in London, and finally serving as part of the garrison in Calais. On the other hand, he was engaged in ultimately unsuccessful legal action over family lands, so it is possible that he might have retired to Wales at some point and led the life of a minor country gentleman had he managed to inherit or otherwise accrue enough resources to enable him to do so.[7]

Above all else, the great volume of material that Elis wrote in the Welsh language testifies to his intense desire to remain intellectually, and emotionally engaged with his mother tongue and the culture it

6. See, e.g., Paul Oskaar Kristeller, *Renaissance Thought and the Arts* (Princeton: Princeton University Press, 1964), 3.

7. Morgan, "Elis Gruffydd of Gronant," 10–11.

transmitted. Words which he himself wrote in his chronicle suggest that he was well aware that he was making a substantial contribution to the Welsh historiographical tradition. After finishing the final narrative section, a discussion of current and recent events in 1552, during the reign of Edward VI, the chronicler concludes his massive work with this colophon: "Da J delych di o veddiant ellis gruffyth sawdiwr o gallis J vediantt tomas vab tomas vab shion vab gruffudd vychan i bantt y llongdy yngwespur, ovewn plwyf llan assaph yn sir y fflint ovewn Tegangyl" (Well may you come from the possession of Elis Gruffydd, soldier of Calais, to the possession of Tomas fab [son of] Tomas fab Gruffudd Fychan, to Pantyllongdy in Gwespyr, in the parish of Llanasaph in Flintshire in Tegangl).[8] This sentence might have served in part as a kind of postal address, directing whomever Elis had charged with bearing the chronicle from Calais to the recipient's Flintshire home in northeast Wales. It can also be read as an articulation of the relationship among the author, his work, and the intended readership. Personified and addressed as "you," the chronicle is presented as a living Welsh entity linking the writer living in Calais with a specific place and an individual reader in Wales.

While Tomas fab Tomas fab Gruffudd Fychan is named in its final lines, the chronicle repeatedly addresses an imagined reader, the rhetorical construct helping to anchor the past being narrated in the present of the act of reading. Elis often begins a section with the noun *Syre,* meaning "lord," "sir," or "sirrah" (though not in the derogatory sense of "sirrah" as found, for example, in many of the plays of William Shakespeare). Other aspects of Elis's narrative style likewise keep an image of his reader foregrounded, urging a continued close engagement with the long work. In at least one place, it is clear that the chronicler intended for his work to reach a plurality of readers back in Wales, defined specially as "men of fine substance and honor," or "[g]wyr o fliant ac anrhydedd."[9]

The suggestion that he came from a comparatively poor branch of a family of *uchelwyr,* or gentry, is borne out by the fact that he sought a career as a common soldier. Elis recorded details of his own military career in his chronicle, some of which are supported by external sourc-

8. NLW MS 3054D, 688v.
9. See the discussion of the chronicle's introduction below.

es.[10] Morgan helpfully summarizes the particulars: "Elis went to Venlo in Gelderland in 1511, to Cadiz under Lord Darcy in the same year, to Fuenterabbia (in Navarre) in 1512, and to Therouanne and Tournay from 1513 to about 1518."[11] He was certainly in military service by the time he was in his early twenties and might have started as a teenager. Despite his being involved in lawsuits concerning family lands in Wales during the 1530s,[12] there is no evidence that Elis ever returned to the country of his birth. He became a servant to Sir Robert Wingfield, perhaps while campaigning on the continent,[13] and was later appointed the overseer of Wingfield Place in London, a position he held from 1524 to 1529 or 1530. The first of his surviving manuscripts, "The Book of Elis Gruffydd," was written at Wingfield Place in 1527.[14]

That manuscript is a miscellany or anthology, containing—like so many of the extant Welsh manuscripts from the fifteenth and sixteenth centuries—a considerable selection of bardic poetry, as well as genealogies, prophecies, and various prose texts.[15] The contents of his chronicle demonstrate that Elis continued to be interested in Welsh bardic culture and traditions relating to poets notable in history or central to leg-

10. Mostyn 158, 669v.

11. Morgan, "Elis Gruffydd of Gronant," 11–12.

12. Morgan, "Elis Gruffydd of Gronant," 10. As Morgan noted, Elis, Siôn ap Dafydd, and Siôn's brother Robert were petitioning the chancery court over their lands between 1533 and 1538. See also E.A. Lewis, ed., *An Inventory of the Early Chancery Proceedings Concerning Wales* (Cardiff, University Press Board, 1937), 115, 123–24.

13. Morgan, "Elis Gruffydd of Gronant," 11. Elis served Wingfield during the 1523 campaign in France, details of which he records in his chronicle (Mostyn 158, 440v–448v). This section of the work has been edited by Thomas Jones and published as "Disgrifiad Elis Gruffudd o Ymgyrch Dug Suffolk yn Ffrainc yn 1523," *Bulletin of the Board of Celtic Studies* 15 (1954): 268–79.

14. This manuscript is also in Elis's autograph hand. On folio 225r he writes, "Elis Grufydd a'i ennedigayth ynGronnant Vcha ym p[l]wy Llanhassaph yn Sir y Fflint a'i ysgrivenodd anno XCCCCCXXVIJ ynn Llundain ymhalas Sir Robert Wyng, yn yr amser hwnw depetti ynghaleis" (Elis Gruffydd, originally from Gronant Uchaf in the parish of Llanasaph in Flintshire, wrote this in the year 1527 in London in the mansion of Sir Robert Wingfield, at that time deputy in Calais).

15. For a detailed description of the contents of "The Book of Elis Gruffydd," see Historical Manuscripts Commission, *Report on Manuscripts in the Welsh Language,* vol. 2, pt. 1 (London: Eyre and Spottiswoode, 1902), 96–103; Daniel Huws, *A Repertory of Welsh Manuscripts and Scribes, c. 800–c. 1800* (Aberystwyth: National Library of Wales, forthcoming).

end: for examples, see "Merlin and the Dreams of Gwenddydd" in part 2 and "Rhobin Ddu" in part 3. The poetry recorded by Elis in his earlier manuscript fills 104 of its 266 large pages and constitutes an anthology of compositions by the most famous Welsh poets from the later medieval period working in the strict cywydd meter (couplets of seven-syllable lines with an end rhyme falling alternately on accented and unaccented syllables and with cynghanedd, internal ornamentation mandatory in every line), such as Dafydd ap Gwilym, Iolo Goch, Gruffydd Grug, Dafydd Namur, Guto'r Glyn, and Lewis Glyn Cothi, and a few poems ascribed to two of the *cynfeirdd,* or "early poets," Taliesin and Llywarch Hen.[16] The remaining contents include a genealogy from Adam to Brutus, "Y Kronickly Byr . . . sydd Esgrivenedic Jr dwyn kof am y xxiv Brenin a varnnwyd yn benna . . . o'r Brytaniaid & Edfeilad" (The short chronicle . . . which was written in order to record the twenty-four kings who were judged to be the greatest . . . of the Britons and the Italians); "The Debate between the Soul and the Body," said to have been translated into Welsh from Latin by Iolo; a tract on the seven planets; "Aristotle's Letter to Alexander"; traditional Welsh prophecies; and a version of "The Seven Sages of Rome," apparently translated into Welsh from French or English by Elis himself.[17] Some of the texts found in this early manuscript, including the poetry attributed to the legendary Taliesin and "The Short Chronicle," presage themes and narratives to which Elis would return at length in his great chronicle.

During his time in London, the man whom he served, Sir Robert Wingfield, became the deputy governor of Calais. As Henry VIII kept no standing army in the modern sense, a position in the garrison guarding Calais was one of the few ways a professional soldier could ensure a salary, and Elis clearly used his personal connection to secure just such a place. He left London in 1530 to join the garrison of Calais, where he seems to have remained for the rest of his life. According to official records of the town, he married a local woman, Elizabeth Manfielde, had children, and bought a house in Calais.[18] In the part of his

16. For Llywarch Hen, see Patrick K. Ford, ed. and trans., *The Poetry of Llywarch Hen* (Berkeley: University of California Press, 1974).

17. Henry Lewis, "Y Seithwyr Doethion," *Bulletin of the Board of Celtic Studies* 2 (1924–25): 202.

18. Morgan, "Elis Gruffydd of Gronant," 14.

chronicle dealing with that year, he records that "ynn y vlwydd o wladychiad y brenin vgain mlynned kyua, yn niwedd yr hron, yr hrynn ysydd y'w ddywedud ar y seithued ddydd ar hugain o fis Jonnawr, J doethum j mewn waedgys o rettunw Kalais, ynn y mann J trigais j o hynny allan, ynn y lle i bum i ynn dwyn vy mowyd y hran v[w]yaf o hynny allan ynn gweled ymrauaelion o bethau ar a uai gymhesur i roddi wynt mewn ysgriuen" (at the end of twenty full years of the king's reign, that is to say on the twenty-seventh of January, I came into the wages of the retinue of Calais, where I lived from that time on, where I have been spending my life for the main part of the time from then on witnessing various things which deserve to be put in writing).[19]

As the final part of the work does include many things that its author witnessed in Calais, the words of the passage above can be taken as a reference to the chronicle itself. Two folios later in the manuscript, Elis notes that he began writing soon after settling in Calais: "Ac ynnol J mi breseddu ynGhalais, myui a ddechreuais nodi kwrs y byd ac ynn vnwedig tyrnas Loegyr, brenin yr honn a oedd yn parhau ynni gariad vyth hryngtho ef a Nann Bwlen, yr hon a oedd yn llidiog jaiwn wrth y Kardinal o Loeger" (And after I settled in Calais, I began to record the way of the world, especially that of the realm of England, whose king was still continually pursuing his love for Anne Boleyn, who was very angry with the cardinal of England).[20] There is good internal evidence, then, allowing us to conclude that Elis began his chronicle in 1530 and finished it in 1552. Given the completely unprecedented length of the work and remembering that he was employed as a soldier, not a full-time writer, it is no surprise that he took twenty-two years to produce this massive text.[21] Even so, as Ford mentions in his translator's note, there are signs that Elis often composed his sentences hastily, an observation that raises an image of the soldier writing furiously during his free time, attempting to get as much in as possible before returning to duty or family.

19. Mostyn 158, 485v.

20. Mostyn 158, 487v.

21. The manuscript, completed about 1552, was bound into the collection later known as Cwrtmawr 1. Like Elis's two other extant works—his "Book" and a translation of medical texts (see below)—it is in his autograph hand.

He completed one other substantial work during his time in Calais, a collection of Welsh translations of English works on medicine.[22] As Elis suffered from illness during the 1540s, his scholarly interest was clearly linked to personal experiences. Consisting of 852 pages, this work would be remarkable in its length if it didn't seem short when set against the more than 2,400 pages of Elis's chronicle. If only the other two works had survived, Elis would be remembered as an interesting but not remarkable copyist, anthologizer, and translator. It is because of his chronicle, the work from which Ford has drawn the narratives presented here, that Elis stands out as one of the most remarkable and significant Welsh-language authors of the sixteenth century.

THE STRUCTURE OF THE CHRONICLE

The sections of Elis's chronicle selected for inclusion in this book can be read as isolated texts, and Ford's lively and engaging English rendition of their prose ensures that they will be appreciated and enjoyed. We will return to them shortly. However, any reader interested in their context should keep in mind that they are part of a long history of the world. It is thus worth discussing in some detail how Elis went about creating this ambitious work and what kinds of influences and sources informed its composition.

The chronicle's early pages have headers in Elis's own hand, alternating between *llyur kynnta o'r vij*, "the first book of the seven," on the recto of each folio and *Yr Oes Gynnta o'r Byd*, "The First Age of the World," on the verso. While this continues through the manuscript's first 270 folios, the practice becomes less consistent and at times confused.[23] The attempt to organize the work in terms of books, most likely stemming from the influence of Ranulf Higden's *Polychronicon*, is then abandoned, and the majority of the work is arranged chiefly

22. S. Minwell Tibbot notes that Elis's main source was Sir Thomas Elyot's *Castel of Helthe*, most likely published for the first time in 1531 (*Castell yr Iechyd* [Cardiff: Gwasg Prifysgol Cymru, 1970], x).

23. See, e.g., NLW MS 5276D, 13r.

according to the *sex aetates mundi,* or, in Welsh, *chwech oes y byd,* "six ages of the world."[24]

It is not only the page headers that use the concept of the six ages as a structuring principle. Dates are commonly given in terms of *oedran y byd* (the age of the world), either *ymlaen* (before) or *ar ol* (after) the central temporal reference point in Christian chronologies, *dyuodiad Krist,* "the coming of Christ."[25] Individual narratives are sometimes introduced with reference to the age in which they happened, as Elis employs phrases such as *ynn yr oes honn,* "in this age [*X* was born or *Y* took place]." The chronicle is a universal history, and the comprehensive scheme of the traditional six ages of the world informed its creation on many levels, dictating the material's general chronological organization and providing a stylistic handle for locating specific narratives within that broader framework.

This framework had enjoyed considerable esteem in Christian historiography for centuries. Some of the most famous thinkers of the early church had shaped its development; indeed, it was founded to a great extent on the ambitious chronological tables of Eusebius of Caesarea (c. 260–350), who synchronized the histories of different peoples. Implicit in his schematization was the assertion that all of pre-Christian history was but a foreshadowing of Christian history. Saint Augustine (354–430) molded Eusebius's chronology into a more developed organization, introducing the ideas of "the great empires" and the *sex aetates mundi.* These six ages were defined as the periods from the Creation to Noah, from Noah to Abraham, from Abraham to David, from David to the Babylonian captivity, from the Babylonian captivity to the birth of Christ, and from the birth of Christ to Judgment Day. During Augustine's lifetime, Orosius employed the six ages framework in his *Historia adversus paganos* (dated to 417–18). Isidore of Seville (c. 560–636) included a chronicle using the *sex aetates mundi* in his *Etymologiae,* a work that had a profound influence on several literary and historiographical traditions.

24. The last page with the word *llyfr,* "book," used in a header is NLW MS 5276D, 137v.

25. Ernst Breisach, *Historiography: Ancient, Medieval, and Modern* (Chicago: University of Chicago Press, 1983), 81–88.

Although Elis sought to record the history of *chwech oes y byd,* the vast majority of his work deals with the final age of the six. Indeed, roughly a third of the entire composition is consumed by the most recent 150 years of history, from circa 1400 to 1552.[26] For the fifteenth century, he relied heavily on two published English chronicles, John Rastell's *Pastyme of the People* (mentioned in "The Origins of Britain," in part 1) and Edward Hall's *The Union of the Two Noble Houses of Lancaster and York.* Many of the narratives in part 3 of this book are from this section of the chronicle. In treating Welsh history, Elis used oral history and folklore, as well as written texts. An excellent example included here is the collection of associated narratives featuring the prophetic bard Rhobin Ddu (see the story named for him in part 3). It seems that Elis had heard tales about this character during his youth in Wales and had seen poetry ascribed to him in other manuscripts. When Elis came to generate his own version of these narratives, published English chronicles treating the wars of the fifteenth century and historiographical and genealogical material contained in Welsh manuscripts also informed his work.

The excerpt that Ford dubs "Owain Tudur and Catherine de Valois and the Rise of the Tudors" is a rollicking and often funny love story. However, in relating this narrative, Elis was also meditating on a matter central to his own identity, for the story highlights the Welsh origin of the Tudor dynasty, which he served. As has been noted already, Elis says that he "put in writing" a great deal of "things" that he himself witnessed. In recording contemporaneous or recent events, he also incorporated information provided by his circle of friends and acquaintances, many of them servants in high places and eavesdroppers in the corridors of power.

But beyond the current events and their continuing effects on history, what the reader of this selection of stories will find most telling about Elis's life and times is the pervasive influence of elements of the supernatural: prophecy, to be sure, but also necromancy, ordinary magic in its many forms, unearthly interventions of many varieties, and the effects of natural phenomena. It is irrelevant to consider Elis's

26. The coronation of Henry IV in 1399 is discussed on folio 279r of NLW MS 3054D, thus leaving more than four hundred folios, or eight hundred "pages," for the following century and a half of history.

belief in such things, for he was a person of his time. It is clear from his treatment of these otherworldly phenomena that he accepted the existence of supernatural intervention in the lives of ordinary people. What is telling, perhaps, is that stories of the kind in this book were not consigned to a separate section of his chronicle but rather recorded as part of the ongoing history he recounts. While we may wonder at the credence given such supernatural interventions in those times, they occurred in the ordinary course of lives lived. It is for this reason, among others, that Ford has indicated the stories' manuscript numbers and folio pages, where the interested reader may, upon examination, find that a particularly bizarre otherworldly experience sometimes directly follows a list of popes or the activities or fate of one of the rulers of the Holy Roman Empire.

Those seeking to identify exact written sources employed by Elis are often frustrated by his tendency to use vague references, which cite only *y llyure,* "the books," *yr ysgriuen,* "the writing," *vy nghopi,* "my copy," *vy awdur,* "my author," or *opiniwn,* the "opinion" of some general group or community of authors or other people. Typical examples are "J mae ymrauaelion oppiniwns mewn llyure yn lloygyr" (there are various opinions in books in England) and "Ynn ol opiniwn hrai o'r Kymru" (according to the opinion of some of the Welsh).[27] Students of literature, history, and folklore alike are at one and the same time excited and frustrated by his imprecise allusion to sources such as *ysdori,* "a story," *kronick,* "a chronicle," and *chwedyl,* "a tale." However, Elis does mention specific references on occasion, sometimes naming a source directly in the body of his narrative (e.g., "megis ac j mae yr awdur Galfriedws yn dangos," "as the author Geoffrey shows"), in the margin (e.g., "darllain ystori Halle," "read Hall's history"), or in a heading (e.g., "Prolog Rastel," "Rastell's Prologue"). The reader who works through the entire chronicle may get the impression that the sprawling composition is set within a complex web of sources and, indeed, is itself a creation woven partly by combining those individual strands and partly by situating something new within that textual web. These sources can be viewed as a complicated network of cultural relationships connecting a variety of texts and traditions. Sitting spiderlike at the center of this vast web is the authorial persona of Elis,

27. Mostyn 158, 283v, 285v.

manipulating individual strands and weaving new ones. As Ford explains in his translator's note, Elis addresses the fact that his various sources do not always agree, and he often challenges opinions voiced by earlier authors.

The narratives selected by Ford often evince a tension, in his words, "between rational history and a cosmology that demands the operation of arcane forces." In a very real sense, Elis's view of history was tempered by traditions that promoted belief in supernatural forces, as we have seen. The Welsh word *brut* eventually came to be used for a traditional kind of historiographical text or textual tradition (the most popular of which was, judging by manuscript evidence from the medieval and early modern periods, *Brut y Brenhinedd,* the "Brut of the kings," the Welsh translation of Geoffrey of Monmouth's *Historia regum Britanniae*). Similarly, the word *brud* came to refer to Welsh prophecies. Both common nouns derive from the proper noun *Brutus,* the name of the first of the legendary rulers whose exploits were chronicled by Geoffrey and others both before and after Elis. During the medieval period and on up through Elis's time, however, the final *t* or *d* in a word was not fixed, and either form could mean either "prophecy" or "text about history." Indeed, as I have argued at length elsewhere, it is best to view them not as two different terms but as one, *brut/d,* which indexes a complex mode of thought in which the past, present, and future of the Welsh and their nation are held in productive association with one another.[28] Elis is at times cynical and dismissive in his treatment of traditional Welsh prophecy in his chronicle. However, in other parts of the same work he suggests that it is possible to engage with prophetic texts and successfully read the signs relating to the future, just as the chronicler can sift through evidence to describe past events.

Several narratives translated here provide some insight into Elis's complex relationship with Welsh historiography and prophecy: See especially the reference to Gildas in "Merlin and the Threefold Death" and the chronicler's musings toward the end of "Gwrtheyrn and the Falling Castle." Also extremely relevant is "Rhobin Ddu."

The most salient aspect of the work's style, and one that provides unity of tone throughout the massive composition, is the presence of Elis's unique and often humorously intrusive authorial persona, very

28. Hunter, *Soffestri'r Saeson*. See also Hunter, "Chronicle of Elis Gruffydd."

much in evidence in the stories presented infra. In a very real sense, this persona can be considered his most original and memorable literary creation. It is manifest in the frequent asides that address the reader directly, sometimes questioning the veracity of a source the author has just paraphrased, flavoring criticism with biting sarcasm, and sometimes providing more general commentary on human nature. In addition to including these comments in the body of his text, Elis glossed his work himself, tempering the high drama of the narratives with humor and cynicism that force the reader to reevaluate the history being related.

The stories presented by Ford in this book provide numerous examples of the ways in which Elis's authorial persona directly addresses the reader. This is a dynamic aspect of the work's style, for, while always instructing and sometimes bringing the reader in close to share a joke or humorous comment about the material in question, he also often rebukes the reader for being willing to believe things that are untrue or "contrary to faith and reason."

As the history moves closer to the present, the closer this authorial persona comes to the foreground as Elis relates events that he himself witnessed, including some in which he played a part. First-person narration had been used before in Welsh literature: medieval love and nature poetry is often cast in the first person (seen in, for instance, the twelfth-century Hywel ab Owain Gwynedd's repetition of the phrase "caraf i," "I love," and the fourteenth-century Dafydd ap Gwilym's fondness for beginning a cywydd with a formulaic narrative anchor, "fal yr oeddwn," "as I was . . ."). However, these poems are expressions of love or meditations on nature and not what Meredith Anne Skura would term "self-writing."[29] In contrast, the later part of Elis's chronicle could be described as the first autobiography in the Welsh language. He details the military campaigns in which he participated, discusses things he witnessed or heard about in the corridors of power in London, and describes aspects of a soldier's life in the Calais garrison in the first person.

One example is his detailed description of his move from London to Calais, one of the major milestones in his life and career. In describing

29. Meredith Anne Skura, *Tudor Autobiography: Listening for Inwardness* (Chicago: University of Chicago Press, 2008), 1.

a dangerous sea, Elis comes to the foreground as a central character in his own story. Although a Protestant convert, he tells us that when a storm threatened to sink the ship, he was one of those who prayed to various Catholic saints, confessing thus: "Addewais i ynof fy hun ddyfod ar fy nhraed a cheiniog i Ddwynwen pa bryd bynnag ar y rhoddai Duw a'r Saint gennad i mi i sathru troedfedd o dir Lloegr" (I promised in myself to travel by foot with a penny for [Saint] Dwynwen whenever God and the saints gave me permission to set foot on the land of England). Elis then presents the reader with some detailed self-mockery designed to make an important theological point about the worship of false idols: "Ac yn y modd yma yr oeddem ni oll yn rhoddi ein gobaith yn fwy i gyffion o gau brenne, y rhain a oedd rai ohonynt hwy ccc o filltiroedd oddi wrthym ni, nog i Dduw ac i'r prenne, drwy wyrthiau Duw, a oedd yn ein cynal ni ar ucha y dŵr" (And in this manner we were all placing our hope more in pieces of false wood, which were, some of them, three hundred miles away from us, than we were [placing our hope] in God and the pieces of wood that were, through God's miracles, keeping us above the water.)[30] The writer becomes his own character, and that character is made both object and subject of his text's morality tale. While a host of kings, popes, and other important people figure prominently in the chronicle, Elis himself emerges as its most complex and human character, often commenting from the margins of history—and writing in the margins of his own work—as a wise, cynical, and humorous bystander, coming to the foreground of the text at times as a hero and at other times as the butt of his own joke.

One of the striking aspects of the chronicle's autobiographical sections is the way in which Elis presents, suggests, and constructs his own identity—always Welsh, at times British (perhaps more in the Welsh sense of *yr Hen Frytaniaid,* "the Ancient Britons," than in terms of common twenty-first-century usage), and at times a proud member of the "English" army. He lived through the Acts of Union (1536–43), which formally annexed Wales to the Kingdom of England, the most obvious manifestation of developments that saw Wales brought more firmly into the grip of the Tudor state. Rather than offer a protesting voice, Elis

30. Mostyn 158, 486r. See also Jerry Hunter, "Poets, Angels and Devilish Spirits: Elis Gruffydd's Meditations on Idolatry," in *Heroic Poets and Poetic Heroes in Celtic Tradition,* ed. Joseph F. Nagy and Leslie Ellen Jones (Dublin: Four Courts, 2005), 765–96.

was one of many Welsh people who enthusiastically entered the service of that regime. In discussing military campaigns in which he—along with a great number of other Welsh soldiers—took part, he describes the force as *byddin Lloegr*, "England's army," or *y milwyr Saesneg*, "the English soldiers," and he was clearly proud of its successes. However, he was also intensely aware of tensions between Welsh and English soldiers within that military community.

In one of the chronicle's autobiographical sections, he describes the disastrous campaign of 1523 in which he participated.[31] Suffering from extremely bad weather in France, some of the soldiers in Henry VIII's army grew unruly. Elis tells us that these men were warned against actions that were "nothing less than treason" (ddim llai no thratturiaeth') and for which they could be executed. Like many of Elis's recordings, re-creations, and fabrications of lively dialogue, his version of the would-be mutineers' collective answer is memorable: "J'r hynn ir attebai y kyuriw wyr gwrthnysig annswynhwyrol drwy ddywedud nad oedd waeth gantheunt twy i krogi yn Lloegyr no me[i]rw o annwyd ynn Ffrainck" (To which these stubborn and senseless men replied that they did not think it worse to be hanged in England than to die of cold in France).[32]

At this juncture, Elis once again becomes a central character in the story he is relating, tossing in substantial doses of humor and self-satire as he assures readers that he witnessed these events firsthand: "Y soon a'r shiarrad hwn a glybu vy meistyr J Syr Robard Wingffild, yr hwn a wnaeth i mi gyuodi o'm gwaal, ynn y mann ir oeddwn J mor gynnes a'r porckell, i wrando yr ymddiuan ac i nodi y kyuriw wyr ac a oedd yn gwneuthud y vugad honn" (My master, Sir Robert Wingfield, heard this rumor and talk, and he made me get up from my shelter, where I was as warm as a piglet, in order to listen to the conversation and note which men where making that noise). More disgruntled talk ensues, leading to the call to return home, and Elis is again forced to leave his warm bed, listen to the soldier's complaints, and do his part to forestall the mutiny. Cleverly contrasting different aspects of his character and his role, he depicts himself as a hapless man robbed of a good night's sleep while emphasizing the crucial service he provided by helping Sir

31. Mostyn 158, 441r–447r. See also Jones, "Disgrifiad Elis Gruffudd o Ymgyrch Dug Suffolk."

32. Mostyn 158, 445v.

Robert Wingfield avoid rebellion in the ranks. Moreover, in introducing the episode, he stresses that Welsh and English soldiers alike were grumbling ("y gwynuan a wnai lawer o'r Saeson ac o'r Kymru," "the complaint was made by many of the English and the Welsh").[33] This may have been "the English army," but the Welsh were a distinct and at times separate group within that mobile military community.

At one point in this extended autobiographical narrative, the chronicler describes how tensions between the army's Welsh and English factions came to the surface in a life-threatening manner. After recording the open cry "to go home" voiced by some soldiers, Elis writes that "everybody was placing the entire blame on the men of Wales, even though twice as many of the Englishmen were even more eager to turn for home than the Welsh" (pawb ynn bwrw yr holl vai ar wyr Kymrv ir bod dau kymaint o'r Saesson ynn chwannogach i droi adref no'r Kymrv). To summarize the nature of the anti-Welsh prejudice that he experienced in the army, Elis draws upon some traditional Welsh wisdom: "Yet, as the proverb is true, 'the dog one desires to kill is the dog who kills the sheep'" (Neithyr, megis ac J mae'r ddihareb ynn wir, "y ki a vynner J laadd hwnnw a vydd ynn lladd y deuaid")—that is, the accusation of killing sheep is used to justify killing a dog that one simply doesn't like.[34]

While serving in London during the 1520s, Elis kept the company of other Welshmen as much as possible, and he often states explicitly that acquaintances from Wales also working in London were the sources of specific rumors and information about goings-on in the Tudor court and other high places.[35] Similarly, while campaigning in France and during his more than twenty years in Calais, he associated himself with other Welsh soldiers. Thomas Jones provides a roll call of these friends and associates: "the spearman, Rhobert ap Rheinallt, from Oswestry . . .; the officer, Thomas Johns, from South Wales; his own cousin, Ifan Llwyd ap Siôn Cyffin, from Llanarmon Dyffryn Ceiriog, who died in Elis's billets; the standard bearer, Siôn ap Dafydd ap Gruffudd from Ystrad Alun; the cavalry man, Owain Gwyn; and many

33. Mostyn 158, 445v.

34. Mostyn 158, 442v.

35. Jerry Hunter, "Taliesin at the Court of Henry VIII: Aspects of the Writings of Elis Gruffydd," *Transactions of the Honourable Society of Cymmrodorion* 10 (2003): 41–53.

others, . . . whom he does not name."[36] We thus glimpse how a professional soldier from Wales who lived most of his life outside that country mitigated the distance from his native land by seeking out and maintaining a Welsh social circle wherever he was. While it can be assumed that these soldiers spoke Welsh together whenever possible, the fact that Elis remained intellectually and emotionally engaged with his mother tongue is overtly manifest in the wealth and breadth of his Welsh-language material in his three surviving works. Although he lived most if not all of his adult life outside the land of his nativity, he wrote extensively in Welsh for a readership back in Wales.

The colophon addressing the chronicle and wishing it a safe trip from Calais to Tomas ap Tomas ap Gruffydd Fychan of Pantyllongdy in Flintshire was discussed above. Elis also included an introduction of sorts, which addresses more than one intended reader, including perhaps Tomas but surely the better-off relatives in Flintshire whom he hoped would help him with his hitherto unsuccessful legal battle. His nemesis in this was Piers Mutton, who had claimed lands that the solider of Calais considered to be his own birthright:

> Ac am vy llauur nid wyf J ynn damuno dim, onid ych kerdigrwydd Ach gair da chwi, A meddwl am y ttrais ar kam a ddaruu y beirs mwttwn i wnneuthud a myui ynn dwyllodrus dan eulun kyuraith Ar kam J mae i ttiueddionn ef yniwneuthud A myui yn wastadol, Ac ynn debig yw wnneuthud oherwydd nad wyf J ynn abyl i ddyuod Jr wlad i ddilin y gyuraith, yr honn gann a glowaf J ysydd gwedi mynned ar gyuyrgoll ynghymru A lloigyr, onid ir sawl a vo kyuoethog J evro dwyllo y gwyr o gyuraith, yr hynn nid ydwyf i yn abyl yw wneuthud.[37]

> And for my labor I do not desire anything, other than your kindness and your good word, and a consideration of the violence and the wrong which Piers Mutton has done continually to me, and is likely to continue to do because I am not able to come to the country to follow the law, which, as I hear, has gone astray in Wales and England, except for the one who happens to be wealthy enough to grease the hands of the lawyers, which I am not able to do.

36. Thomas Jones, "A Welsh Chronicler in Tudor England," *Welsh History Review* 1 (1960): 15.

37. NLW MS 3054D, 2r–v.

Elis continues this wordy appeal, denouncing a lack of "justice" (*kyuiownder*) and beseeching these readers to intervene on his behalf, stating that he would do the same for them where they in need and he in a place to do so. He concludes this introduction with a poignant sentence: "Hyn a ddaruu J mi i sgriuenv hrag mynned y matter drosgof ynn llanhassaph" (This I wrote lest the matter be forgotten in Llanasaph).[38] While referring directly to his claim on lands in Llanasaph, Flintshire, these words can be extended, as Morgan suggests, to all of "the matter" discussed in the long chronicle.[39]

Whatever the nature of the exact "matter" that Elis wanted remembered in his old parish back in Wales, there is no mistaking the fact that the earlier part of this introduction describes the material contained in the work: "Nid wyf i ynn kymerud arnnaf amgennach no gwr sympyl disas diddysg anwybodol a vai ynn kymerud arno vod ynn ben llongwr i lywio ac i gyurwyddo llongiaad o wyr o vliant ac annrhydedd dros vor llydan i wlad ynn yr h[o]n ni biasai neb o honnunt twy irmoed ynn y blaen" (I do not pretend to be anything more than a simple, rustic, uneducated, unknowledgeable man who would pretend to be a captain steering and guiding a ship full of men of fine substance and honor across a wide sea to a land where none of them had ever been before).[40] In describing his massive chronicle as a new "land," he suggests that he knew full well that Welsh readers had never before encountered such a work in their native language. As is common in introductions to works from the medieval and early modern periods, the author ceremonially debases himself before his readers, protesting that he is unworthy, while suggesting the opposite by presenting a work clearly considered to be worthy of interest. However, the specific metaphor that Elis employed in his introduction is extremely significant for several reasons, not the least of which is that it reminds us that he sent this novel and ambitious contribution to Welsh literature back to Wales from across the sea. Perhaps more significant is what it says about how he regarded his ambitious project. Couching self-praise in ritual self-debasement, this sentence also stresses that the chronicle's Welsh readers could not travel to this wondrous new land without Elis. Thanks to

38. NLW MS 3054D, 2v.
39. Morgan, "Elis Gruffydd of Gronant," 20.
40. NLW MS 3054D, 688v.

these new translations by Patrick Ford, readers who can't understand Elis's original Welsh prose will nonetheless be able to visit some of the more interesting and memorable parts of that vast and fascinating literary landscape.

THE TRANSLATOR AND HIS WORK

Patrick Ford has long been interested in Elis and his chronicle. In 1977 he published *The Mabinogi and Other Medieval Welsh Tales* (also from University of California Press).[41] Among other things, that book presented readers with the first modern English translation of "The Tale of Gwion Bach" and "The Tale of Taliesin," two associated narratives that he translated from Elis's chronicle.[42] These stories describe how supernatural powers were acquired by Gwion Bach, later reborn as the poet and culture hero Taliesin. In addition to containing memorable episodes such as the shape-shifting pursuit of Gwion Bach by the witch Ceridwen and Taliesin's defeat and humiliation of Maelgwn Gwynedd's court poets, these linked stories provide a lively Welsh parallel to Irish narratives describing the acquisition of poetic inspiration.[43] This makes it no surprise that Ford's translation has become a mainstay in the study of Celtic literature and is surely one of the many factors that have kept his popular 1977 book in print for more than forty years.

While poetry associated with the legendary character Taliesin survives in earlier manuscripts, prose tales of Gwion Bach and Taliesin first appear in a work written between 1530 and 1552, Elis's "Cronicl Chwech Oes y Byd," or "Chronicle of the six ages of the world." In preparing the present book, Ford has returned to Elis's chronicle to provide readers with a wide selection of narratives about magic, prophecy, and related themes in translation, the vast majority of which have never been available in English before. The contents provide an exciting

41. For an edition of the original Welsh text, see Patrick K. Ford, ed., *Ystoria Taliesin* (Cardiff: University of Wales Press, 1992).

42. The first English translation was published by Charlotte Guest during the second quarter of the nineteenth century. Also discussed in Patrick K. Ford, *The Celtic Poets: The Songs and Tales from Early Ireland and Wales* (Belmont, MA: Ford and Bailie, 1999).

43. See Ford, *Celtic Poets;* Joseph Falaky Nagy, *The Wisdom of the Outlaw: The Boyhood Deeds of Finn in Gaelic Narrative Tradition* (Berkeley: University of California Press, 1985).

introduction to the variety of narratives found in Elis's long chronicle, including his unique treatment of subjects from literary traditions with which the reader will most likely be familiar, as well as a great deal of traditional Welsh tales.

The value of these Welsh narratives cannot be overemphasized. Some were surely folktales, transmitted orally and heard by Elis when he was a child or young man in Wales. Others he perhaps gleaned from older manuscripts that have since disappeared. For example, "The Tale of Taliesin" mentioned above is not the only traditional story involving the ruler Maelgwn Gwynedd found in the chronicle. There is also the lively story that Ford titles "Maelgwn Gwynedd, His Wife, and the Ring." While it contains international folktale motifs that help scholars situate it within a broader context of tradition and oral transmission, this specific Welsh tale is not recorded in an earlier source. Indeed, Elis's chronicle is *the* most valuable early source for traditional Welsh narratives after the medieval manuscripts containing the *Mabinogion* tales. Readers of this new book will see why.

Jerry Hunter

Translator's Note

This project began in the spring of 2019 when I conducted a small reading group for graduate students in Harvard's Department of Celtic Languages and Literatures that explored the stories recorded by the sixteenth-century historian and scribe Elis Gruffydd. Thanks to the availability of the his manuscripts online from the National Library of Wales at Aberystwyth, the students were able to gain a degree of fluency in reading this rather difficult recounting of the *sex aetates mundi*. By the time COVID-19 brought our group activity to a close in early 2020, I had decided that there was plenty of material in Elis to fill a book with translations of some of the more arcane narratives in the manuscripts. The stories of Merlin, including his peculiar origins and prophecies, were immediately attractive to me, as were those of the strange birth and remarkable career of Arthur, king of the Britons. But there were many other stories that also dealt with the magical arts of necromancy, vaticination, and other means of dealing with the unseen world and the future, and these matters affected historical figures from the earliest times to the reign of Henry VIII, when Elis's chronicle concludes.

I owe a debt of gratitude to those graduate students, whose enthusiasm—together with their sense of humor in dealing with a difficult-to-read manuscript—inspired me to continue with the present work. Professor Jerry Hunter, whose splendid introduction to Elis prefaces this collection of translations, has been with this project from the beginning. I am indebted to him for his willingness to stay with the project throughout its development and indeed his enthusiasm in commenting on the translations as they progressed. It has been more than thirty years since he and I independently encountered Elis, and we have held on to him ever since.

These stories deal with mythical and legendary figures from ancient times, as well as historical figures from late antiquity and Dark Age Britain and known figures from medieval and early modern Wales and England. In all of these stories we see a conflict between rational history and a cosmology that demands the operation of arcane forces in the lives of people. Elis often expresses his disbelief in the latter and yet assiduously records accounts of magical and other supernatural forces. A quick search by readers will reveal many books and treatments in other media of stories about Merlin, Arthur, and related figures. Many of these are serious historical or fictional accounts based on English, French, or other continental sources. We are not competing with that history and fiction; rather, we are using a single source to illuminate a sixteenth-century historian's view of a great amount of material available to him from a variety of both written and oral material. These and other aspects of Elis's treatment of his materials are discussed in detail in Professor Hunter's introduction.

I have attempted to represent Elis's work with as little authorial interference as possible. My aim has been to give the reader a feel for Elis the chronicler by retaining some of the more peculiar elements of his style. Nevertheless, the translator must intervene at times for the sake of clarity. Elis uses very little punctuation, virtually none, so that it is difficult at times to know where a complete thought begins and where it ends or where the next thought begins. This fact is exacerbated by his use of pronouns as relative markers. The paratactic style allows for "sentences" to go on and on at great length, often frustrating the sense. To combat that, I have normalized the text by introducing punctuation according to modern norms. Elis uses capital letters at times, but these do not always introduce new "sentences." Elis sometimes indicates a change of subject matter with a sizable indentation of the first line of the new narrative direction. He is also very fond of parallelisms, repeating nouns, adjectives, and verbs with their synonyms; this trait has been carried through into the translations. The business of translation is further complicated by the apparent haste with which Elis compiled his chronicle. The meaning of a passage is sometimes frustrated by a loss of continuity in sense, as if he had forgotten where he was going with a thought. Apparent haste has also led to the loss of a letter or letters in certain words and the insertion of extraneous letters in others. The spelling of Welsh in Elis's day was not normalized as it is now. In modern Welsh, *yn wir* means "true"; *anwir* means "false." In Elis the first of these might be spelled *ynnwir*, the latter *annwir* or *ynnwir*, so that for the translator "true" or "false" often depends on context. Elis's sense of economy in the use of full pages meant that he often crowded separate words together or broke a word between lines. These habits can be frustrating at times, especially for inexperienced readers.

The following passage illustrates some of these peculiarities. Line lengths are as they are in the manuscript. Imagine that each line extends the width of the page:

> Or herwydd arachos y kymerth diacklessian
> ddiruawr lid a soriant mawr wrth y verched ac yn
> wir nid heb achos ac yn vnwedig am wneuthud y k
> y uriw vurn ysge ler o vewn y ly ys ef ac yn n y l l
> id yma megis ac y maer ysdori yn dangos y my na
> ssai y brenin ddien yddu y holl verch drwy a ngau
> dybryd er hroddi shiampyl y eraill yr hynn nis god
> e uai rai oi gyng gor y ddo y wneuthud na myn pa
> ri yddo dynnu y veddwl ai amkan oddi ar y ffordd
> yr yd oedd ef yn darparu drwy gyngghori yrbrenin
> yr kadw dyuiown der y gyuraith y hroddi wyntt me
> wn y sgraff heb na hwyl ynllyw nag ang gor ar ni
> a fferi y vorwyr gymerud y lless dyr hwn ar merch
> ed yn ddo ai ar wedd ef yr moor gymaint a sshi wr
> nai llong dan hwyl gy maint a diwyrnod a noss wa
> ith.

NLW MS 5276Di, 77v (see "The Origins of Britain" for a translation)

As the introduction notes, Elis had access to a number of more or less contemporary chronicles and histories, among them Welsh, English, French, and Latin, to which he refers and from which he often quotes. These accounts do not always agree on historical matters, and Elis does not ignore those disagreements. More than that, he does not hesitate to challenge the disparate accounts of the same events. But despite these challenges, he strives for common ground, often concluding that "it doesn't matter" whether it was that way or this, because the result or outcome was the same. His critical handling of his sources is well illustrated throughout these texts.

Elis took many of the stories that follow here from English and Welsh sources—not surprising, given that he was a Welshman and was employed by the English, as the account of his life in the introduction details. But his chronicle also draws upon a broad spectrum of material, from ancient Greece through biblical times to his own day. The present work is organized to show the scope of Elis's interests and work, and it must be stressed that its organization is my own: the stories here do not necessarily follow one another in the manuscripts. The first part exemplifies Elis's treatment of antiquity and then the first age with material from Genesis, from the Creation to Noah. From there, we move to the early Middle Ages, with stories of Merlin and Arthur, and on into the late Middle Ages and the influences of magic and the other arts on the lives of known historical figures, especially the Welsh princes and English monarchs. For those readers who may wish to consult the originals, I have indicated the manuscript sources and folios throughout the texts. There are four manuscripts: National Library of Wales MS 5276D, parts i and ii, and MS 3054D, parts i and ii. They are in the public domain and are available online from the NLW. The frontispiece is a digitalized picture of one of the manuscript pages, produced by special arrangement by the NLW for this book.

Patrick K. Ford

The Texts

I

Earliest Times, Ancient and Biblical

THE BIRTH OF HERCULES

It will be apparent that this story, belonging to Greek mythology, bears a strong resemblance to the birth tales of Merlin and Arthur, and that is not surprising. Heroic births are no doubt common to all cultures and share many features. It has long been noticed that such stories occur in the many language communities of the Indo-European family of languages. This and the following tale belong to these traditions. (Also see the note to "Owain Tudur and Catherine de Valois and the Rise of the Tudors" in part 3.)

NLW MS 5276Di

(41r) At the time when Jupiter was ruling as the king in Crete, there was a great marriage in the town then called Thebes, whose king was Creon. The marriage was between Amphitryon and the maiden Alcmene. The story says that she was one of the fairest and most elegant maidens in that part of the world. The king of Crete and Juno his queen and sister were invited to the wedding and the feast. If one can believe the work of the ancient authors, Juno was a woman steeped in the arts and learned in the several sciences that people call sorcery and necromancy. During the feast, Jupiter looked intently at the face, form, and bearing of Alcmene. Juno watched this closely, for she could see how the flame of the fire of love for Juno had turned his heart into a burning torch, for she could see that he could do nothing but look at the newly married woman.

Juno became very jealous over Jupiter and Alcmene, but she discreetly kept her composure, and shortly after the wedding feast Jupiter and his queen returned to Crete. There, because he couldn't get Amphitryon's queen out of his mind, he began to converse with his queen and a squire of his who was called Gamides. After a long discussion about her Gamides said that she surpassed all the maidens and women in that part of the world in beauty and (41v) shape and decorum, saying that there was not a king in that part of the world, regardless of his power, for whom she would not be a fitting mate. Because she was surpassing in beauty and virtue, the story says that hearing such great praise for her caused King Jupiter to lose his color. The queen saw this, and from then on she became so jealous about her husband and Amphitryon's queen that from the rage and fury of her jealousy she determined from that moment to destroy Alcmene. Indeed, if the story can be believed, after the conversation of the squire, love for Alcmene grew more and more in the heart of Jupiter.

Around this time, enmity grew between the king of Thobe and the king of Thebes and war broke out. Jupiter offered support to one side and Amphitryon supported the other. But as the story goes, no sooner had these two kings come to the battlefield with their two forces than peace and concord came between the two kings. And so the field was abandoned and all of the soldiers went home. The kings prepared to take leave of one another, and after each of them said farewell to the other they each went on their way. King Amphitryon departed first, as Jupiter saw. Quickly, he took his squire Gamides, and they mounted their horses and followed the route that was closer by two days than the route that Amphitryon had taken to his court. It was through a desolate area with precipitous mountains. But it was not unlikely that in his love and desire to see the sight of Alcmene, his body was not stinting to take the pain, and so he traveled this route night and day until he and his squire came around midnight (42r) to the gate of the castle where Alcmene was. He immediately called to the porter, who got up from his bed and opened the window so that he could see the two by the light of the moon, looking like King Amphitryon and his chamberlain. They said that that is who they were, for through magic he had made them look like King Amphitryon and his squire. After some discussion the porter let him in, and he awakened the people who were in the queen's chamber. They let him in and greeted him as their master, as did the queen. Immediately, he was embracing, kissing, and fulfilling his desires with Alcmene throughout two nights and a day. When he supposed that King Amphitryon was getting close to home, with his magic he vanished from among the queen and her people, took up his horses, and urged them on swiftly toward home.

As the story says, no sooner did the king of Crete vanish and begin his journey than King Amphitryon came home to his castle and to his queen. This stunned the queen and her people, and not without reason. But still everyone kept the secret, especially the queen, who kept everything hidden from King Amphitryon. Some time after this journey, word came to the king of Crete and his queen that Alcmene was pregnant. This made the queen of Crete add an ill feeling to the old jealousy, supposing in her heart that it was her spouse who was the father of the child, for Juno had counted the time from when the aforesaid battle ceased until the end of nine months, all the while (42v) thinking to herself how through her magical arts she might destroy Alcmene and her pregnancy. She labored nightly in her two sciences, necromancy and sorcery, in which she was very skilled, and in enchantment or magic or charms. And when she saw that Alcmene's time for delivery was near—for she had been keeping track of the time—she asked the king of Crete for permission to make a pilgrimage on foot secretly from Crete to Archianos to make an offering to the temple of the goddess Diana. The temple was connected to the castle where Alcmene was dwelling. Jupiter agreed to this readily, for he had no idea of her intent. Soon thereafter she began her journey on foot, like a poor woman, and she kept going until she reached the temple. There she made ardent addresses to the goddess Diana. At that time a number of women and maidens of the queen of Amphityron would come to pray before the image of the goddess to give deliverance and to ease the burden of their mistress. They made chants and prayers that Juno heard and noted carefully in her heart. And then, trying to get more information about Alcmene's situation, she rose to her feet, and like a shy and humble woman she addressed one of the handmaids, whose name was Galatia.

After greeting her she said, "Aha, noble woman, were it not for modesty and shame I would ask you a question." The maiden invited her to ask whatever she wished to ask. To deceive the maiden she said, (43r) "I have wandered so much of the world that I do not know where

I am standing, so I want to ask you to tell me the name of the temple and in what country it stands." The maiden replied, "You must know that you are within the temple of the goddess Diana beside the castle of Amphitryon, to whom the temple belongs as well as this castle, which is called Archiens and stands between the city of Athens and Thebes." Then Juno asked the maiden, "Isn't it here where Amphitryon and the queen Alcmene keep their court?" Galatia explained to her that it was there that they dwelt most of the time. She then asked the maiden what pleasures they enjoyed, telling her how she had heard tell of much goodness about them both far and near. The maiden thanked her in careful and courteous words for her kind words about her master and mistress, saying that they were happy, except that her mistress at the moment had taken to her chamber and had begun her lying-in and was awaiting the time of her labor.

As soon as the maiden departed from her, Juno sat on the ground in a corner of the temple, facing the image and with her legs crossed. From that position she began to make various devilish chants and charms to the goddess and to the lofty lords of her arts to prevent the queen from delivering her burden. During this time, Alcmene (43v) remained in her labor and her travail, her legs crossed in the same way as Juno sat in the temple. Although all the women and maidens were around her in her travail, she indicated great pain, because however the women lifted her, whether upright or sitting or reclining, her legs remained crossed, despite what they would do to her. And Juno kept her in this anguish and position with her arts and magic for three days and three nights in order to destroy Alcmene and her pregnancy. You must know that the temple of Diana was not empty or without some of Queen Alcmene's friends praying and beseeching the unresponsive image to deliver her of her burden. Meanwhile, a number of these maidens saw the figure of a woman sitting in the temple with her legs crossed, but sometimes in the shape of a bitch, sometimes other foul or monstrous animals, as if she were pleased to change her image to disguise herself lest anyone recognize her.

Finally, after much anxiety, Galatia supposed that there was some cause hindering her mistress from delivering. She was thinking about the images of things that the maidens said they had seen in the temple. She took a number of women and maidens who were attending the queen and led them to the temple. There they all fell on their knees before the image of the goddess, with all of them pretending not to see the figure of Juno. They lifted their hands toward the firmament, saying in loud voices, "Most worthy through great praise and honor be your name, Goddess Diana, immortal goddess, over the face of the entire earth, for in this hour you have sent deliverance to Queen Alcmene from the pain she has suffered in her travail for nearly three days and three nights, for in this hour (44r) she has found deliverance of the most beautiful son one has ever seen."

As soon as the figure heard these words she sprang up and ran from the temple in the shape of a wild cow, from rage at hearing the news about Alcmene. Thereupon the women and maidens returned and raised Alcmene and arranged her in the way one ought to arrange a woman who was at that stage. And very soon after that she was delivered of her burden, from which was born two sons. Then Galatia and her assistants knew that it was through the arts of necromancy that their mistress was prevented for so long from delivering. But they didn't know who was responsible.

As the story relates, the firstborn of these twins was very solid of body and limb. The other one was weak and pathetic. The stout one was named Hercules, whom they said was the son of the king of Crete, and the other one was named Epeclitus, who was said to be the son of King Amphitryon.

Indeed, from this birth all the countries and the people of the land exulted and rejoiced greatly. But Juno had not left the area, turning her thoughts on how best she could destroy the children. In the end she complained within herself in this way, atop the Olympian mountain, where she spent most of her time after leaving the temple, as previously said: "Aha, O powerful and knowing gods, what does it benefit me to be from the blood of Saturn and a noble lady wearing the diadem of the queen of Crete upon my head and taking pains with mind and thought to (44v) learn all the worldly arts that exist and brought to mind, when the goddess Diana is so cruelly against my will and against the working of my arts."

And when she finished disparaging the might of the goddess and reviling her ill luck and misfortune in various ways and at various times, she determined to conjure two poisonous serpents. They came to her swiftly, thanks to the excellence and strength of her art. She led these from the Olympian mountain to the castle of Amphitryon. There she searched about from one place to another until she came to the wall of the nursery. By means of her art, Juno kept herself and her serpents hidden until it was the dark of night and everyone in the nursery was deep in sleep. Then she pushed the serpents into the chamber through a window, ordering the evil creatures to kill Epeclitus. When they had done that, they slithered toward the crib of Hercules, where they each took one side of the crib, aiming to destroy the child. But the boy seized a snake by the neck in each of his two hands and squeezed them tightly, screaming fiercely until the keepers woke from their sleep. When they saw that Epeclitus was dead and heard Hercules, who was screaming in his crib and had turned his face toward his struggle with the serpents, they too began screaming loudly. But as the story says, before the people had time to lift up the infant, Hercules had strangled the two snakes.

At the time there were two kings in the castle at Archianus who had come to visit Alcmene. They were Euginus, the king **(45r)** of Athens, and Estrius. They and all the other people were told the story of the death of the one son and the victory of the other. The story recounts that they all marveled greatly over that and especially about Hercules's great victory. And to magnify this feat and on the advice of the two just-named kings, Amphitryon took this marvelous boy and a great number of his nobles and his regular attendants and went from there to Athens, accompanied by the kings and the two serpents, to sacrifice to Mars, the god of battles, and to give praise and glory to his image in honor of the achievement of Hercules. Of course, the news of this feat traveled widely across the face of every land both far and wide. And so when men of those lands heard that they were bringing the boy to Athens to offer the snakes to the aforementioned false god, many of them flocked to Athens to see the wonder. A great crowd had gathered by the time the kings brought the boy there. Because of the throng that was in the temple trying to see the boy and the snakes by the time each of the kings had made their offerings, the kings asked Amphitryon to place the boy and the dead serpents on a high place in the temple, along with men to turn and display the boy and the results of his action to the people on every side of the temple, so they would be able to see the boy. And the story says that at that time he was about ten days old. The serpents were wretched and repulsive in appearance, and as a result the entire crowd celebrated the boy's deed, all except Juno, who with the fury of her nature opened her mouth **(45v)** wide and at the top of her voice spoke as follows: "Honorable nobles and commoners, I beseech you to look at the foolishness of King Amphitryon, who believes in his heart that Hercules is a true, natural son of his by his queen Alcmene. But in reality there is not a drop of his blood in the body of the boy you see there. Indeed, there is not one person in this assembly who knows Jupiter, the king of Crete, who cannot consider and realize without doubt that with respect to the strength of the little boy's body, his bearing, and the bravery of his deeds, that he is really and truly the son of the king of Crete."

THE BIRTH OF ALEXANDER

NLW MS 5276Di

Another tale of prophecy, shape-shifting, and the darker arts. The child born of this union has features unlike those of his mother or father and, indeed, unlike those of humans and more like those of the animal to which he is compared. The meaning of the child's name, "defender or protector of man," either was known to Elis from his sources or perhaps is a contribution of his own.

(145v) As for the history of Alexander, some of the accounts say and claim that he was the son of Phylip, the king of Macedonia, by his queen Olympias. But this is untrue, for he was a bastard, borne by the queen as follows more clearly in the present work in writing.

At some time before this there was a king ruling in Egypt named Neptanabus. He was a man very learned in each of the two arts known as astronomy and necromancy. Various kings rose up against him and conducted fierce wars within his realms. By virtue of his arts he could see clearly that he could not stand against them or oppose them with either men or arms and so he dressed himself in the garments of an astronomer, and in this way he fled secretly from Egypt to Macedonia. There he took service in the court of Phylip, the king of that land, as a learned astronomer. The story says that he was able to reveal the truth about many things that would come to pass.

(146r) The story says that not long afterward this King Phylip went to war and left Neptanabus there with the queen. Soon after the king left, the queen implored Neptanabus to tell her her fortune, which he promised to do. He told the queen as follows: "I see in the course of the stars in the firmament that the powerful god Amon will come unseen and will lie by your side, and from him you will become pregnant with a son. And so you must be prepared for the god Amon." In this way, through his art, he came to her chamber to see her and fulfilled his desire on her. She became pregnant and told this all to Neptanabus, who knew the matter and the story as well as or even better than she herself did. But nevertheless he said, "Look now, you will believe what I have told you in the course of time."

Soon she began to grow heavy and drew near her time, which frightened her very much, for fear that the king would get word of her pregnancy and become furious with her. And so to explain the situation, Neptanabus sent a clever letter to King Phylip explaining how the god Amon came in the form of a dragon to his bed and to the queen, whom he made pregnant, making it clear that the queen was very upset about it all.

It wasn't long before the king returned to his court and to the queen. She, out of modesty about her misfortune, could not look the king in his face but kept her eyes down every day. **(146v)** The king perceived this and asked her to be cheerful, telling her, "I know the reason for your modesty and your embarrassment. We have to be contented and take everything happily, for neither I nor anyone can oppose the will of the gods."

A short while later, as the king and queen were taking their ease, Neptanabus entered the hall in the shape of a fierce dragon, and boldly he laid his hand on the queen's belly. The king said, "Truly, I saw this dragon as I stood on the battlefield against my enemies, and at the time I felt in my heart that it was the god Amon."

Very shortly after that, Neptanabus caused an egg to appear in the lap of the king, who took the egg and flung it to the floor, where it broke. Out of it came a young dragon, which wandered around the shell, trying to find a place to go. So the king went to the philosopher Amphiton to ascertain what this vision signified. After some time he explained to the king that the queen had given birth to a lad who would be the greatest and most superior man in his time, but who would wander the entire earth. And in his next return to his native land he would die at the height of his fame and his honor. At the time of his birth there was upheaval and tumult in the firmament from thunder and lightning from which arose a tempest of hail, each stone of which, the story says, was as big as the egg of a goose, the likes of which no one had ever heard mention since the beginning of the **(147r)** world up to that time.

It was during this tempest that a child was born to the queen, a child who, as the story says, was very unlike either the father or the mother, for his hair was curly and one of his eyes was marbled with various colors, while his other eye was black. The toes of his feet were pointed like a lion's claws, which justifies his name, Alexander. When he had grown to a certain age, King Phylip gave him to Neptanabus to learn the arts of astronomy and necromancy. Alexander spent some time with his master and true father, a fact unknown to King Phylip or to Alexander. As the story says, he used to go night after night to the top of a high mountain, near the place where Neptanabus dwelt, to learn the arts from his master.

THE STORY OF THE ROOD

NLW MS 5276Di

This narrative was widely known throughout the Middle Ages, when it was also called "The Story of the Rood." It is not in the Bible, though the setting is Genesis. The text appears early in NLW MS 5276Di, where the first two pages are badly damaged and the narrative cannot be followed with any clarity. The story becomes legible on the third page. As we know from other tellings of the story, Adam and Eve have been expelled from the Garden of Eden and have had three children. It is interesting that Elis is critical of Moses, the supposed author of the first five books of the Old Testament, whom Elis reminds us was born long after the events recorded here.

(3r) [Adam speaking:] ". . . the path I followed for me and your mother when we came out of Eden was bare and naked without fruit of the earth growing beneath our feet from that moment to this day." As I understand it, Seth undertook his journey by following that path until he came before the gate of Eden, or Paradise. Immediately, he encountered the angel that was guarding the gate. Seth explained to the angel how his father, Adam, had told him to come there in all haste to fetch for him the oil of mercy. According to the story, the angel responded quickly to Seth in detail that his father, Adam, would be dead by the time he returned to his dwelling. Then the angel instructed Seth to bury his father, giving him three seeds or three kernels, and with these instructed Seth to place them under the base of the tongue of his father's body as he put him into the ground. The angel told Seth that a beneficial tree would grow from these seeds, saying that his father would receive the oil of mercy and come back to Paradise on the day when that tree would come to full fruition. Seth believed those words to be true, and at that the angel suddenly vanished from him.

Thereupon Seth returned to his dwelling, where he found his father dead on the ground, as the angel had said. Seth buried him as the angel had instructed him, putting his father's body and bones to rest, putting the three seeds mentioned earlier under the base of the tongue of Adam. According to the story, three excellent saplings grew from the mouth of Adam. Concerning the power and virtue of these seeds, this work will discuss extensively in various places and at various times as the moment requires.

In this way, the holy patriarch ended his life, having lived it in pain and adversity and sorrow for as long as 932 years. But even so, some of the learned ones have shown in their books that Moses left out of his book as many as one hundred years of the total. This says that Seth son of Adam knew clearly in his day what the total number of years was before Moses was born. And for this reason it is said that Seth experienced sorrow and grief, and so this story says that he wept bitter tears for a long time in the place where he toiled. At that time he called the place the Glen of Lamentation. It lies adjacent to the glen or valley called Glen Ebron.

THE TOWER OF BABEL

NLW MS 5276Di

This narrative about the building of the Tower of Babel and the subsequent confusion of tongues appears in Genesis 10 and 11, where it is simply and briefly recounted. As there was no Welsh Bible at this early date (William Salesbury's translation of the New Testament appeared in 1567; the whole Bible by William Morgan came in 1588), Elis must have used other sources, both Latin and vernacular, such as Saint Augustine's *Civitas Dei* (see the introduction). One is left to wonder what influence this treatment in Welsh of this wonderful story had on the Welsh Bible that was yet to come. The events recounted here occur in the wake of the Flood and the movements of the descendants of Noah's sons.

(10r) After they conversed at length about the matter, they agreed on a date to meet in the land called Shinar. After each of them had assembled their peoples, the three leaders and their followers convened: namely, Jactan son of Eber, who was the head of the line of Shem; Nimrod, who was the chief of the line of Ham; and Sulfen, who was the head of the line of Japheth. They discussed ways of deceiving the Heavenly Father, for they could see clearly that there were the same kinds of sins among them at that time as had been among the people in the first age of the world, sins that prompted the Father to destroy them all for their wickedness and their foul sins. After a long discussion, lest God send similar punishments upon them because of their sins, they decided in their counsels to set men to work to build a tower of brick and mortar from the stuff of the earth to defend themselves and their people in case of a similar punishment and to get knowledge of the Father's plans, for their thought and intent was to build this tower as high as the heavens so that they could overhear every word the Lord said.

Indeed, the twelfth chapter of the first book of the Bible says that these three leaders did have such a tower built. But that book does not say they built a tower as tall as twenty-one miles high, as popular opinion says. But the holy book shows and maintains that the Heavenly Father looked at the corruption and foolishness of these leaders and their three hosts and that their unending vain trust in worldly cunning was tempting Him to destroy them.

We are given to understand that at this time there was but a single language among all of the people of the world and that language was Hebrew. As punishment upon the people for their vain and foolish plan, the Lord put confusion upon their tongues and on their way of speaking. This happened suddenly among them, and the Lord made their one language into many languages among them. This happened equally among peoples of all lands, in their houses and their dwellings, and also among the various people who were working and exerting pain and effort in building the tower. The confusion chiefly affected those who were working on the tower and especially such people as had conspired to construct it. In an instant the Lord distorted the words of the people so **(10v)** much that the workers on one scaffold could not understand or know what a man who was on a scaffold above them or below them was saying. So when one of them asked for mortar, the other would bring him a rock, because not one of them could understand the other. After they stared at one another in astonishment for a long time, they all wondered what sort of disaster had befallen them. They had to abandon the work and come down from the tower. After mingling and milling about, they discovered that some of them spoke the same language and could understand one another. They quickly gathered with others who spoke the same language and set themselves apart from the others.

At the time, as the story shows, there were as many as twelve and sixty lineages, and the Lord made each of their individual tongues unintelligible to the others. Indeed, the story says that there was not a single person among all these lineages whose family did not experience this punishment from the Father. Only the house and family of Peleg son of Eber was excepted, for among the family of his house the Hebrew language remained uncontaminated. In the view of Saint Augustine, what we see here is the widely disseminated notion that continues to show the uprightness of Peleg and his steadfastness in embracing exemplary virtues and reminds us that he had not agreed with the leaders and the aforementioned peoples about building the tower.

Furthermore, some of the accounts say that this tower was twelve and sixty stories high when the Father twisted the tongues and that the people on every level of the scaffolds did not share a common language and so had to leave the work and come down to the ground. According to this story, as soon as they had come down to the ground and were standing on the earth, seven miles of the tower sunk into the ground and then seven more miles fell down before their eyes; seven miles of the tower still stand. But despite this account, neither the Bible nor any of the ancient authors write about or mention these matters.

THE ORIGINS OF BRITAIN

NLW MS 5276Di

John Rastell (1475–1536) was an English writer and historian. The destruction of Troy and the subsequent move by Aeneas and other surviving Trojans to Italy that he recounts is familiar to us from Vergil's *Aeneid*. In conveying this brief history, Elis reveals doubts about the facts of Rastell's story. He then turns to the origins of Britain and the tale of Diocletian and his thirty-two daughters. And as is his wont, Elis contrasts wonder and marvel with truth and reality. There is perhaps no other text in this massive chronicle where he attacks in such detail the credibility of the narrative he relates.

(76r) There follows here the prologue to a book of chronicles by a man named John Rastell, which he called *The Pastimes of the People* and which begins as follows: No doubt every learned man has read the stories and chronicles by various authors in various languages and a multitude of noteworthy accounts that confirm in some detail how Aeneas of the White Shield and his son Ascanius, along with a great many people, came to Italy shortly after the Greeks destroyed Troy. Aeneas and his people were welcomed in Italy because of the discord and war between Latinus, the king of Italy, and Trusolun, the king of Turkey, and also because Aeneas was a descendant of Dardanus.

In the end, after much time, Aeneas became the king of Italy after Latinus, against the will of a number of the nobles of Italy. These men wanted Lavinia daughter of Latinus to marry one of the Italian nobles, but Aeneas won out over all of them and ruled as king after Latinus, his father-in-law. After Aeneas, Ascanius ruled for seven years. After Ascanius, his son Fulvius was the king **(76v)** of the Latins. According to some of the stories, Ascanius was the son of Aeneas by Lavinia, though others say he was the son of Aeneas by a daughter of Priam, the king of Troy. I have never heard of anyone able to sort out the truth about this; rather, every reader holds with the opinion of his author, and so I will not belabor the matter further; rather, we will turn to discuss matters that we had begun to talk about earlier, for all the authors agree unanimously in saying that it was from the man called Ascanius who was the king of the Latins or Italy after Fulvius that Romans like Romulus and Remus came.

Concerning this island, Britain, there are various opinions in writing. Some of the writers say that learned men had a name for this island before it was either founded or settled and that because of their learning they called it *clas Myrddin*, "Merlin's folk," but despite that none of them has said, as far as I can determine, anything about the word *clas* or what it means.

It is well known to every reader of each of the two languages that both the Welsh and the English chronicles agree that there was a man called Diocletian who, the story says, was the king of Syria. He had thirty-two daughters, and these were married on the same day to thirty-two kings. (77r) Within a short time after these marriages, the wives became very unpleasant in nature and their actions turned evil; they increased their hostility, becoming surly and refusing to submit to their husbands. Finally, the men came to the king and complained bitterly to Diocletian, their father-in-law, of all the faults and rebelliousness of his daughters, their wives. The story says that the king prepared a great feast to which he invited all the men and their wives. The next day King Diocletian called all his daughters into a room with only himself and his daughters. He spoke in a kindly and tender way about their faults and the complaints of their husbands. He chastised them sternly for their misbehavior, urging them to improve their ways and submit to the will of their husbands or lose his affection. But despite his fatherly counsels, they did the opposite. As soon as the daughters learned how their lords had complained against them to their father, that they were women of an accursed nature, their evil dispositions grew and grew hour by hour and day after day from that time on. The story tells how after discussing it, they agreed in their rage and anger to kill their husbands as soon as they had the opportunity. When they found them all asleep one night, each of the wives took a knife and cut open the men's veins.

Diocletian became enraged at his daughters, and indeed not without cause, especially (77v) for committing such an atrocious act within his own court. And in his fury, as the story says, the king determined to punish the daughters with a horrible death to set an example for others. Some of his council did not approve of that; rather, they caused him to change his mind and advised him to preserve the justice of the law by putting them all in a ship with no sail, no rudder, and no anchor. Sailors were to take that vessel out to sea as far as a ship under sail could travel in a night and a day and then leave it there, without power, with the women on board. And so the king sent his daughters out to sea, where the sailors left them. It is not likely that the women could enable the vessel to travel the seas, even if they had the materials and the equipment. Still, the story says that after long travail, through toil and trouble, they came to land on this island. At that time, the story says, the island was empty, wild and devoid of people. Finally, when the women had turned the soil here and there and especially in the area where they (78r) had come to land, they supported themselves with meat and honey and fruits of the earth. Soon their natures began to burn with desire and emboldened their flesh and their hearts until they did not know how they could have the company of men. So devils came in the form of men by taking bodies from the firmament and men's nature, lost in distant lands through pollution. With this seed they coupled with the women, who then became pregnant by these false spirits.

Now some people remember with effort the story that says that Albion was the name of the oldest of these daughters and that she ordered her sisters to name this island Albion after her. The name survived for some years after that until the time when their descendants who were in their wombs arose and grew in age and strength and multiplied and made more children, who after a number of years grew into an evil and ungodly tribe, huge in size and strength. They were called giants, and from them this island was called Ynys y Cewri, "Island of the giants." They kept that name from that time until Brutus came to inhabit this island.

This story displays much more of wonder and marvel than of truth and of reality, and yet it has survived among the Britons and the English, who accept it and embrace it instead of true and accurate history. Because of that, other peoples and nations of other languages laugh (78v) mockingly at our foolishness and our folly for putting credence and trust in a story and fable as farfetched and as unlikely to be true as this story. As any intelligent and thinking person can well see after long consideration and thinking, it is a great wonder for any man anywhere whose natural reason governs his thinking and his discernment to put credence or trust at all in a story such as this. There is no historian in the world who can say with certainty who was the original author of this account. Nor can they say from whom it was passed on, nor the name of any scribe of authority from this country up to the present day who ever wrote this story.

Moreover, we have never seen in written books in other languages nor heard from a single reader of histories of other languages and foreign realms that there was ever a king called Diocletian in Syria, nor mention of a story like this. Surely, if this story were true it would have been recorded by some of the writers or authors from that part of the world or at least by writers or authors of other countries near to Syria. It makes sense that in every country there are learned men of various languages at the present time who have devoted themselves through work and study to recording stories and histories that are less full of wonder and less likely to celebrate them in writing than this story. Every sort of reasonable man can easily determine that this story is untrue, and that for two reasons: One is that it is unlikely that the king of a country would have (79r) as many as thirty-two nubile daughters ready to marry as many men at the same time or in a single day, as this story claims. And just as unlikely as that is the likelihood of finding thirty-two widowed kings to marry these women in a single day. And it is just as unlikely to be true that so many wives are so unnatural and so hateful toward their husbands as to conspire to commit an act so evil as to murder them all in the same night, as the story claims. It is peculiar too that not even one among so many women was of a reasonably good nature, who out of courage and love and affection toward her husband would reject a deed as evil as this and save the life of her husband. Furthermore, it is unlikely for a vessel or ship to be able to move across so much perilous sea without sail or rudder, as the story claims, without hitting land or landing anywhere until it arrives at this realm. This is difficult for a man to believe, especially the kind of man whose opinions are guided by reason and faith—above all, knowing that this journey of over three thousand miles on the seas from Syria to this island is a route in which there are many narrow and perilous straits between islands, where it is difficult for a vessel to pass unharmed. And yet despite that, there was not and is not from that day to this and never will be any way to avoid and (79v) evade such places. Every ship that comes from that part of the world must pass through the narrow waters and the aforesaid perils before they come from Syria to this island. In their way there are many rocks and sandbars and constant seas where one is likely to come to land in many places before reaching the sea that surrounds this island.

People who are expert and learned in the *mappa mundi,* the chart or image of the world, and in the science of cosmography understand and see all the obstacles and constraints and perils along the way of such a sea voyage and the distance between this island and the Kingdom of Syria. Also, it is true that this story stands with neither true faith nor sound reason. What is really striking is for faithful Christians to trust and believe in their hearts that devils could couple with women and sire children in them in the way the story says. For if it is true that devils or false spirits had that sort of power and ability at that time, why can't they have the same ability and power to do the same thing today, at least among the faithless ones who don't believe in God? God does not unmake anything he made in those first six days of the world, and it is true that there is no mention today anywhere in the world of such a race or breed as this story (80r) describes. What is more, if God had given these spirits or devils such power and means that they could do such things, still I do not see any reason for their offspring or their children to become huge giants, exceeding other men in strength and size. It only makes sense that the seed from which they grew and the way it was sown was no different from the kind of seeds or fluids from which children grow and are nurtured in the womb of mothers today, tonight, and always, and so I see no reason or cause for them to be different in strength and overwhelming power than the children born of a man and a woman. Therefore, in my mind and estimation the story is nothing but wickedness and mockery.

This island was never called Albion after the name of the woman in the story. Rather, some of the masters say in their histories and remind us that the island had been called Albion for a long time. The name came from and was put on it from expressions and words of foreign speakers for the white slopes, cliffs, and rocks that surround most of this island, especially the southern and eastern parts of the island that border the sea. When the weather is clear and open, these cliffs can be seen clearly across the sea from distant lands because of the whiteness of the color. And so it is likely that some of the Latins coming near enough by either land or sea to these areas could see the white cliffs along the borders of the island. Because this island at that (80v) time was strange and unknown to these people and they had had no word for it, they called it Albion, after the white cliffs, for *albus* in Latin means "something white." It is likely that this is how the island was first called Albion, and afterward the Britons called it *ynys wen,* "white island."

After a considerable growth of knowledge of the form and way this island first took the name of Great Britain or the Island of Britain, there is much and varied discussion. But the general opinion holds that it was after the name of Brutus son of Fulvius son of Ascanius son of Aeneas of the White Shield, who came from Troy to Italy, as this work has shown. This Brutus was the first man who inhabited and dwelt in this land, which after his name and his people was called Island of the Britons or Island of Great Britain. As his story shows, it was not previously inhabited except by the occasional giant. This idea or story is widespread among the Welsh and the English because of the work and the authority of the man called Geoffrey of Monmouth. He wrote his history in the time of King Henry, the second of that name after the conquest of William, Duke of Normandy, who was the king of England around the year of the age of our Lord Jesus Christ 1069. As his prologue shows, Geoffrey made his book or history, which he says he **(81r)** prepared for Robert, Earl of Gloucester, the king's uncle, affirming that the story was true, saying that the archdeacon of Oxford, Master Walter, had brought him the history in an ancient book that was written in the old language of the Britons and had lain in a library within the town for many years before. Geoffrey also says that Master Walter asked him to read the book and tell him of its contents, as he was a Welshman. In the book, as the prologue states, was the story and the history of the women just recounted here. Geoffrey translated the book from Welsh to Latin, including the stories of Brutus and many of the kings of this realm, to educate the English about the beginnings of the habitation of this island. When the book was ready, he gave it to Robert, Earl of Gloucester, as mentioned before.

But despite all this, Geoffrey gives neither the name of the ancient book nor the names of any of the writers or authors who wrote the story in Welsh. This was and is considered by men of learning to be a major fault in a scholar as good and as sensible and as prepared as the books show that he was. And yet despite these peculiarities and objections within the stories, Geoffrey's work may yet be true. The English, however, in their sophistry bring these objections before us like dust to blind our trust and acceptance and to get us to believe, as most of them do, that neither the women mentioned here nor Brutus were ever in this realm. The history book **(81v)** that the English put their trust in and give the most weight to is the one called *The Commentaries of Caesar,* which Julius Caesar wrote with his own hand during the time when he was conquering France, Ireland, and this island and making them subject to Rome and the Romans. That was about forty-eight years before the birth of our Lord Jesus Christ, a time when the aforementioned person, Caesar, made a great effort with considerable care, as the work shows, to find true knowledge of the origins of habitation on this island and also to describe its shape and form, the nature of its people and the land. He shows the position and size of the island, with the nature of the estuaries and the way the major rivers flow to the sea. Then he speaks of the customs of the people in every part of the land. Yet he never makes mention of Brutus. Indeed, the book shows that though he made a careful effort in asking old and young during this time, he was still unable to get accurate information about who or what sort of people first settled this island. Furthermore, Gildas son of Caw of Britain wrote a great book of history called by the English *De gestis Britonum* [*De excidio et conquestu Britanniae*]. This was about the year of the age of our Lord Jesus Christ 600. Also, Saint Bede of England wrote (82r) a large history, which the English call *Historia ecclesiastica gentis Anglorum,* around 730 years after the birth of our Lord Jesus Christ. And neither of these two authors offered any evidence that Brutus was the first inhabitant of this island.

At some time and period the island was named Great Britain, and Saint Bede says firmly in his history that the first inhabitants of this island came from Armorica, which today is called Little Britain, and so they named this island Great Britain. Nor can anyone find in the chronicles of the Romans and the Latins that there was a King Postumus or Silinus who had a son called Brutus who killed his mother and father, as Geoffrey says in his history. As a result of this, most scholars suppose that if this story of Brutus had been true, it would have been written in either the chronicles of the Latins or those of the Romans. These authors preserved in their writings many of the things worth remembering and fewer matters of wonder to look at than in this history, and they included all the kings of the Latins in their histories and especially Latinus, Aeneas, Ascanius, and Fulvius and such kings as succeeded them and all their children and how they ended their lives in this world, and yet there is not a word about Brutus.

Furthermore, this Geoffrey did not claim or say in his history that all of Gaul was full (82v) at the time of the siege and destruction of Troy. But a number of authors in various languages show that these lands were full of people long before the time when Brutus was supposed to have landed in this realm. And so, many of the learned scholars believe that his history cannot be true; rather, they insist that it is not possible that this realm was vacant and devoid of people from the beginning of the world until the time when Brutus and his people are said to have inhabited it. Of course, the whiteness of these tall cliffs on the shore and especially around Dover on that side of the island are and every day were standing opposite their faces and in full view of the people who dwelt in the northern part of Gaul. And from Dover to the nearest part of Gaul there was no distance or journey on the sea from one shore to the other that a ship or skiff could not sail in less than three hours. Therefore, it is likely that people from that land were the first who ever landed on this island, and it is likely that they did not allow the island to remain empty or vacant from the beginning of the world until the coming of Brutus. Because of these and similar reasons, most of the learned men of the world take Geoffrey's story as false or (83r) foolish. Because he is a Welshman, the English and other nations think that it was to honor and glorify his people that he wrote his history, out of his head and on his own authority, because they could not find a book with this story written by any authors before Geoffrey.

Still, despite all the various reasons why these authors reject the work of Geoffrey in their various histories, I will neither reject it nor deny that it is true. In the same way, I will not affirm that any of this history is true and correct. Although men of other peoples and lands both far and near take these histories as foolishness and nonsense, I will not let this history be forgotten without bringing it forward and writing it in this work just as Geoffrey told it in his history—and indeed, not only to give confidence and learning to anyone to believe and trust firmly that this history is true but also to provide further knowledge and learning to people who may take the trouble to read this dense work. Here is the pith and kernel of this history and many of the histories of other countries and lands and other times, so that the readers may understand and listeners hear and understand the many notable examples of various kings and nobles about their goodness and nobility in ruling their realms and their kingdoms through great virtues of sense (83v) and feelings of love and affection for the commoners who have praised and honored them for their nobility and their goodness.

This, then, is a mirror for princes and kings of every realm and country, to look at and to follow examples in ruling their lands. Also from careful reading of this book, the reader can fully see and understand how the Lord punishes those princes and rulers everywhere in the world for their wrongs and their evil lives, through war or death or starvation, and sometimes they are punished with all three of these at the same time, especially when the princes and nobles devote themselves to pride, anger, and jealousy and have neglected God's grace and his law and have taken pride and pleasure in evil and wicked deeds.

God also sometimes punishes the people for the misdeeds of the princes—especially when they devote all the desires of their flesh to the sin of fornication, whereby they have acted carelessly and heedlessly about keeping the rule of righteousness between weak and strong—to succor the fully impoverished, to enable them to have a life in truth and under law, and to punish the proud ones for their oppression and theft and deception. The Father of Heaven devised and ordained that kings and princes of this world preserve and maintain his law among all. I will demonstrate all this in the present book in more detail when the time and opportunity arise.

II

Merlin and Arthur

THE BIRTH OF MERLIN THE PROPHET

NLW MS 5276Dii

The name *Merlin,* from the Latin *Merlinus,* is attributed to Geoffrey of Monmouth (*Historia regum Britanniae*). The Welsh name is *Myrddin,* also spelled *Merddin.* It has been suggested that the change from the Welsh form was due to Geoffrey of Monmouth's concern that English and French speakers might confuse the first part of the name with the French *merde* (shit), an unhappy coincidence. It is interesting that Elis cannot account for the phrase *clas Merddin,* one of the early names for Britain in the Welsh triads, in the preceding tale. The Welsh *clas* refers to a community of men, as in religious orders, so this would seem to mean a community associated with Merlin: prophets, men of arcane powers. The town Carfyrddin, modern Carmarthen, was also thought to be named after Myrddin, though that etymology has been shown to be false.

This story is brutal, with the third daughter unable to escape the fate of her sisters; despite her religious zeal, the devil wins again. Her offspring arrives fully developed and is lowered down in a basket to a holy monk, who raises the child, a beginning reminiscent of the epiphany of Taliesin, who was set adrift in a basket in the water.

(298v) About this time, as authors say, there was a nobleman living in south Wales beside a town called Caerllion-on-Usk, as some of the books hold, but others contend that it was beside a town called Caerfyrddin that he lived. As the story says, he was a very religious person, and his wife was of **(299r)** the same noble descent and also devout. The story says that they had three daughters, all of whom, as the story says, suffered great misfortune, for the devil got each of the two eldest pregnant, one after the other. And so each of them was buried alive, for the law at the time required that punishment for anyone who became pregnant except through marriage. Shortly after this, the father and mother arranged for the third daughter, whose name was Aldan, to enter the temple of Peter the Apostle to take religious vows. The father and mother were so tormented by these events that they died by their own hands, by hanging.

It wasn't long afterward that Aldan, the third daughter, became pregnant in the temple while keeping her chastity and her vows, through the malice and wickedness of the devil. She was soon brought before the law to be questioned and reveal the truth as to the father of her pregnancy. She told them in so many words how a young man, as it seemed to her, came to her in her chamber when the doors and windows were shut tight, in the dark of the night. "It was he," said the maiden at last, "who made me pregnant," telling them about several occasions when she did not know where he came from or where he went. Upon those words, she was sentenced to death, according to the law and custom that held on this island at the time. Present there and listening to the sentence and the judgment on the girl's life was a man of great sanctity and holiness, whom **(299v)** the monastery said was a man who knew her mother and father well. And so he petitioned the judge and the legal authority to give him permission to keep the girl until the time came for her to deliver the child. After some discussion, they agreed with the monk. He placed her in a strong tower to keep her, with women and maidens to tend to her and plenty of food and drink for them and every sort of need that pertained to a woman in her condition, closing the doors tight so that none could come to them and they could not get out. The women were ordered to tend to Aldan and her burden without fail when her time came, instructed to take the child born from her body, wrap him in cloth, and carefully put him in a basket and release him through a hole or window of the tower.

When her time came, Aldan gave birth to a male child, who, the story says, was as hairy as an animal and ready to walk. He was hideous and had an unpleasant look about him that caused one of the maidens to moan loudly to herself about the appearance of the child, saying, "It's sad and a pity that someone as pure as your mother should suffer death for bearing such an uncivilized and unpleasant creature as you are. And in my view and estimation, you are not the offspring of a man, because I have never heard that the natural offspring of a man and a woman is ready to walk the moment he is born, only you." At these words, so the story says, the child **(300r)** replied as follows: "Don't be concerned about the punishment of my mother, because I will answer for her and will keep her innocent in this matter."

This statement greatly shocked the woman and the maidens who were in the room. But anyway, as soon as the woman took care of him and sent word to the monk, she put him in a basket, and with a cord through the window she lowered him to the ground, where the monk was ready to receive him. The monk took him immediately to the house of the justice, who, upon the request of the monk, sent for some of the lawyers to listen to the youth talking as he exonerated his mother, by showing them how one of the evil spirits, the one called the Scoffer, deceived his two aunts one after the other, intending to bring him into the world, and then finally, "as devil he deceived my mother, Aldan, who after long labor brought me into the world." And then he showed them various signs to convince them that the Scoffer was his father, to the point that they could not go against a single reason that he was giving on behalf of his mother. And from his arguments she got her life back.

Following this, the monk had him baptized and named him Merlin. And then he released Aldan and set her free from her prison and gave her son to her to raise, which she did lovingly thenceforth.

MERLIN AND THE THREEFOLD DEATH

NLW MS 5276Dii

The motif of a threefold death is well known in folklore the world over and can take many forms. The present narrative is designed to allow Arthur to prove to his court that Merlin's prophecies are real and that he does indeed have the power to foretell the future. What is interesting here is that one of the king's entourage devises a plan to prove the efficacy of Merlin's prophetic powers. The story also accounts for the arcane nature of prophecy and Gildas's role in the difficulty in understanding the meaning of the myriad images designed to cloak the real significance of the prophecies and prophetic dreams of Merlin.

(342r) There follow here certain prophecies that Merlin made to Arthur, by whom he was held in high esteem in the early days. Because of that, as the story goes, some of the king's court grew jealous of him, so much so that they convinced the king that Merlin was nothing but an empty-headed fool and that he could no more foretell the future than anyone else. To prove it, one of them told the king in some detail that at the next lodging where the king and his men would stop as they made their way to the north of the island, he would pretend to be ill. The king agreed quickly to the knight's plan. He also let some of his court in on the plan.

And so the king proceeded on his travels from monastery to monastery. At each stop, the first knight to arrive apprised the abbot of the plan, and by the time the king and his court arrived, the knight was lying ill in bed. The abbot grieved bitterly to the king that one of his nobles was sick and likely to die. The king went to look at the man, taking Merlin with him. After spending a few moments with the man, Merlin told the king and the abbot that they needn't worry about the man dying just now, that he would not die in bed from a sickness; rather, that he would die from hanging.

(342v) At the next monastery the man was ill with a venereal disease. The king, the abbot, and Merlin all came to look at him. After some time, Merlin told them that the man was not going to perish from a sickness but that he would die of a broken neck. At the third monastery, the man pretended another illness. The king, the abbot, and Merlin came to look at him. Merlin said that the man was not going to die in bed; rather, he would die from drowning. These were three tragic deaths, which not any single man could perish from. According to the story, the news spread throughout the court, and everyone began to be bored with Merlin's prophecies. He soon saw this, and so, as some of the books tell us, he remade many of his earlier prophecies and confused them in such a way that it was difficult for anyone to understand them from that time on. But some of the other books claim that it was the saintly preacher Gildas son of Caw of Britain who confused the prophecies so that it was now difficult for anyone to understand them until he made it clear to them. At the time, Gildas was preaching to the British, whom he saw believing more in the prophecies of Merlin than in the words of God. And that was why he made those prophecies more difficult for anyone to understand.

But it doesn't make any difference who made them difficult to understand, because most authors agree that it was done to make them unintelligible.

Anyway, the story goes on to say that the aforementioned knight was riding hastily over a bridge when his horse stumbled in its stride, and the knight was thrown over the horse and over the bridge, where one of the knight's feet was caught, and so he was hanged, and in the fall he broke his neck and fell into the water. And in this way, the knight was hanged, broke his neck, and drowned. In that way he suffered the three deaths. (343r) And thenceforth, men would seek the company of Merlin and his prophecies, even though they were more difficult to understand than before. And the story says that Merlin made many more prophecies at the request of Arthur, as the record will show further on in this work.

MERLIN AND THE DREAMS OF GWENDDYDD

NLW MS 5276Dii

Merlin's sister, Gwenddydd, appears elsewhere in the early Myrddin poems and in Geoffrey of Monmouth's *Vita Merlini*. She is at times a prophet in her own right, but in this story she is visited by prophetic dreams and must have them explained or interpreted by her brother. Merlin is depicted here as a type of "wild man," living in nature, experiencing periods of irrational nature, cautious about food and drink. The relationship between him and his sister also serves as the background for the brilliant novel *Gwenddydd* by Jerry Hunter, which won the prose medal in the National Esteddfod of Wales in 2010. At the end of the first paragraph here, we glimpse something of Elis's work ethic: he keeps going with "useless" material only to keep busy!

(395v) According to some authors, there was a man living in the land called Nant Conwy around this time, and his name was Morfryn. But others say that it was Morfryn Frych, prince of Gwynedd, (396r) which cannot be, according to the poems. But anyway, the text says that a man of this name had a son, called Merlin son of Morfran, and a daughter, Gwenddydd. And according to the story, the boy's mind was unbalanced, because one moment he was irrational and lacking basic sense and the next he'd be in his right mind and would be wise and intelligent and ready with answers and good counsel for anything that was asked of him. God had given him the gift of the spirit of prophecy, and these prophecies he would reveal in metrical form when he was in his right mind—and especially to his sister, Gwenddydd. And the writing in front of me says that she was wise and learned and compiled a large volume of his sayings, especially those prophecies that pertained to this island. Some of these follow here in the present work, though there isn't much useful sense to be gleaned from most of them. Still, to keep busy, I will copy down all those I have seen in writing.

The books tell that this Merlin was so unbalanced in his mind that he refused to live in normal houses, especially during the three months of summer, but rather lived in mountain caves and in huts he made from leaves in the valleys and forests on both sides of the river Conwy. His sister would often visit these sites and places with food for him, which she would leave in a place where he could get his provender when he came to himself. At times, so the story goes, it happened that Gwenddydd experienced certain strange dreams on some nights. These she retained intact in her head until she saw the time and opportunity to relate them to her brother, Merlin. On these occasions she prepared bread and (396v) butter with leafy herbs from wheat bread, with various drinks in a variety of vessels, each drink in the state its nature required. So wine was in silver, mead in horn, beer in a wooden mug, milk in a white bowl, and water in an earthen jug. All these she arranged in order beside the food inside the leafy hut where Merlin would come when he was in his right mind, to take his sustenance.

A short while later, as the story says, he returned. Meanwhile, Gwenddydd had hidden inside the leafy hut or cell to listen to his comments. And then, as Gwenddydd relates in some detail, Merlin took up his fine sandwich, to which he addressed a number of stanzas, in which he said that England will not make war everywhere, because you don't eat a sandwich from the middle. And when he had eaten some of the sandwich, he complained about drink. At that, Gwenddydd appeared before her brother and showed him the order of drinks as she had set them out. Then Merlin asked his sister what sort of liquid was in the bright shining vessel. Gwenddydd replied, saying, "This drink is made from vines of the earth and is called wine." "Aha," said Merlin, "this drink is not suitable for me or for my people, because the nature of this drink is to make the rich who regularly imbibe it here poor." And then he asked Gwenddydd what sort of drink was in the horn. She replied as follows: "This drink is made from water and honey and is called mead by our (397r) people." "Aha," proclaimed Merlin. "Much of this drink is not healthy for me or anyone, because its nature is to make the healthy ill." And then he asked his sister what sort of drink was in the colorful wood. She answered, saying, "This drink is made from water and grain and is called beer." "Aha," exclaimed Merlin, "none of this drink is good for me, for its nature is to steal sense from the wise." And then Merlin asked Gwenddydd what drink was in the white bowl. She answered, saying, "This drink is created from the output of animals and is called milk." To which Merlin said, "Indeed, this drink is good for me and my ancestors, because it is natural for nurturing the weak and helping the frail and strengthening the meek and increasing the grit of the strong." And then he asked what drink was in the earthen jug. Gwenddydd said, "This is one of the four elements and is called water, which the Heavenly Father sent to nurture man." Merlin then said, "You have spoken truthfully, and this is the one best drink that I'll drink to slake my thirst till Judgment Day."

After this, Gwenddydd asked him to listen to her relate some of her dreams to him, dreams she had experienced on certain occasions in the past, asking him to analyze them and show clearly what they meant. And so Merlin asked her to relate the dreams, which follow here in writing in this book.

The First Dream

My loyal and dear brother: last night in my sleep I imagined as if real that I was standing in a big, broad field which appeared to be full of small piles of rocks. And moreover, there were large piles among the small ones. And I could see a great number of people continuously taking rocks from the (397v) small piles and throwing them onto the big piles. And yet despite this I could see neither the small piles getting smaller, no matter what I saw of people making many trips, nor the big piles getting bigger, despite how busily the people were carrying stones from the small piles and throwing them onto the big piles. And from the strangeness of the dream I awoke, but indeed I was not able to get the strange dream out of my mind.

How Merlin explained the dream to his sister

Gwenddydd, my beloved sister, don't wonder too much about your vision, because you won't suffer from it. Understand that the field you saw signifies this island, and the small piles represent the farmers of the realm and its laborers at every single level who live legally and win their bread through labor, trusting only in God. The big piles signify the lords of the land of each and every rank and grade. The people you saw carrying the stones from the small piles and throwing them onto the big ones represent the servants or agents of the lords, who are always ready to employ their servants to take away constantly and endlessly what the farmers and laborers have produced, sometimes claiming authority of the law and sometimes by plunder or by outright theft. And inasmuch as you did not see the big piles getting bigger, despite all the activity you saw of people carrying stones from the small piles to the big ones, that demonstrates the wrath of God and his anger, because God will not allow the wealth to be taken away so unjustly to enrich the takers and their heirs. And as you did not see the small piles diminish, even though you saw stones removed from them, that represents the grace of God and his mercy, because **(398r)** great is his power over nobles of every grade as well as over ordinary farmers for their earthly condition. And yet despite this, no matter how much harm the nobles and their minions do to them, the common folk will be neither worse nor poorer, for as much as they lose in that way, God will send them twice as much another way, especially if they suffer such oppression patiently and without complaint and by entrusting punishment and vengeance to the Heavenly Father, to whom the punishment of every evil is fitting and proper, for it is he who ordains the weak and the strong. And indeed, no matter how much the pure of this world may lose, God can furnish the needs of mortal man in this world and of the many pure ones in the world to come. And there you have what your dream signifies.

And after this, she told him the second dream, beginning like this:

My wise and dear brother, I had a second dream. In my sleep I imagined that I was standing in a grove of alder trees of the noblest and fairest that man can conceive or imagine. Then I saw a large group of men armed with axes approaching. They cut down the alders and struck the wood down from their roots. In an instant I saw that the straightest and most beautiful yew branches one could imagine were growing out of the roots of the alders. And from the wonder of all that I awoke, and from that day to this I cannot get that image out of my mind.

How Merlin explained the second dream,
saying as follows:

Gwenddydd, my advice to you is to not be too troubled by the dream, for there is no damage or harm to you from it. The grove of alder trees you saw signifies this island and its ancient people, who are impoverished greatly and especially by the nobility, represented by the alder grove. As (398v) you saw, the alders, the nobility, are all destroyed. But despite that, just as you saw the yew springing from the roots of the alders, so nobles will come from the remnants of their line. At that time, no wealth will remain in the hands of this new generation, whose own offspring will wed below their class, and from these will come forth capable native Welsh, who will endure for a long time after. And there you have the meaning of your dream.

Then she told the third dream, saying as follows:

My dear brother, a third dream came, and in my sleep I saw myself standing on a round, level ground, on which I could see a great number of mounds and lofty shining thrones. And in my mind and my perception, I saw the earth shaking until the thrones fell onto level ground, in place of which, in my mind and perception, there suddenly arose piles of leaves, and on these mounds I could see different kinds of sweet-smelling flowering plants growing. There is great wonder in my heart from that dream ever since then.

How Merlin explained the third dream, saying:

Dear Gwenddydd, don't be concerned in this matter, because the vision will not harm you. The round, level ground represents this island, and the mounds represent the nobles of the island. The earthquake shows that war will come to destroy all the privileged ones, just as you saw the destruction of the thrones. The mounds of leaves which you saw rising immediately in their place show that their riches will come or descend to ordinary men. The flowers that appear will grow from these powerful evil nobles, perhaps to the fifth generation, and each of these will possess the **(399r)** hearth of his father, his grandfather, and his great-grandfather, and then they will disappear like filth from a dung heap. And there you see the meaning of that dream.

And after this she revealed to him how she saw
a fourth dream, saying:

Merlin, my brother, I imagined in my sleep one evening that I was standing in an enclosed field of the finest wheat a man might ever see with his eyes. The ears of the wheat I could see fully ripe and the stalks pure green. And I saw a huge infestation of pigs surge through the hedge and break into the field, where they wreaked destruction and devastation on the wheat until it was completely flattened. And then I saw a pack of white greyhounds coming into the wheat field. They ran at the pigs and killed them all. I have not yet recovered from that sight.

How Merlin explained this dream, by saying:

Fair Gwenddydd, don't worry about this matter, for the field of wheat represents this realm, and the wheat signifies the people, and the ripe grain and the stalks show the men young in age with their hair white at this time, which would indeed be as strange a sight as seeing ears of wheat fully ripe and the stalks not yet strong. And the pigs you saw breaking into the field of wheat indicate that a mighty plague will come to this realm, which will destroy people in the same way as you saw the pigs ruining the wheat. And the greyhounds show that men will come as greyhounds that will avenge the cries of the white-heads against the pigs, which the greyhounds will drive from this land.

(399v) After this she revealed the fifth dream
to him, saying:

My brother, I saw this fifth dream. I imagined that I was standing in the middle of an exceptionally large cemetery, which I saw was full of girls or young maids. And I saw that they were all pregnant and near to birthing. And I imagined in myself that the offspring were conversing with one another from their mothers' wombs. This is a great wonder in my heart when I think about it.

Then Merlin said, "Don't let it disturb you,

for the cemetery signifies this island, and the girls or maidens signify that a world and time will come when matches and marriages are made among heirs at a very young age. And indeed, everyone even less of that age and generation will marry very young, and the children and heirs that are brought forth from these will be full of wickedness and cunning. And as much as you imagine that the children speak from their mothers' wombs, that shows that a child of fifteen years will be wiser in that time than a man of sixty years at the present time.

This is the end of the dreams.

MERLIN'S PROPHECY AND THE REIGN OF CASWALLDAN

NLW MS 5276Dii

The form of the name *Caswalldan* is peculiar. *Caswallawn* is well known in the early Welsh pedigrees and would seem to be a regular development in Welsh of the Latin name of Cassivelaunus, the British leader who opposed Caesar's invasion of the island. Caswallawm Lawhir was said to be the father of Maelgwn Gwynedd, but in "Maelgwn, His Wife, and the Ring" (see part 3), the name of Maelgwn's father is Caswalldan Lawhir. The *d* in this name may represent a phonetic development in Elis's northeast Wales dialect.

(410v) After the death of Cadfan son of Iago son of Beli son of Rhun son of Maelgwn Gwynedd, according to the two eloquent authors Guido and Geoffrey, Caswalldan was crowned the king of Wales in the year of Christ 635. This was around the first year of the reign of Dagobert, the king of the Franks. This Caswalldan was, as the story says, a victorious man who won a number of towns and castles from the Saxons. Geoffrey says that he was so cruel against the Saxons that he had many destitute people killed and whenever he came upon a pregnant Saxon woman he had her womb cut open and the infant she was carrying cast out. In **(411r)** this way, with monstrous cruelty, he overcame Penda, the king of Mercia. Then he took his hosts and went to war against the West Saxons. Cynwacus raised a great army of his people to oppose him, and after a time he encountered the Welsh king Caswalldan beside an arm of the sea within the West Saxon kingdom. Caswalldan gained the upper hand over his enemy, sending the king fleeing and killing countless numbers of his forces. Then, as the story says, Caswalldan had some throwing machines made to drive the enemy to the sea, and as many as he could seize he held as prisoners. The story then says that he took his forces to western areas and led them from there into the territory of the king of the city of Caer Gangen, and after a period of fighting and battles he destroyed him and his kingship. As a result of that, Caswalldan became very proud of himself, to the point that he had an image of himself made in bronze, which he had set in a rock next to the port that is now called Dover, to unsettle his enemies and make them fearful, for that is where the Saxons frequently came to land. This is the man of whom the prophet Merlin spoke in his prophecy:

> The wombs of mothers will be split from the place where children are born before their time. In that time there will be great pain upon men which will avenge his wrongs to the needy, and the man who would do those things will cloak himself in a mask of bronze and be seated upon a bronze horse, which will protect the gates of London for a long time.

And as Merlin's prophecy says, Caswalldan had many brass and bronze images of himself made and set in various ports and harbors within the realm, as well as at the gates of the city of Caer Ludd, to make his enemies nervous and fearful. These allowed him to overcome them with his own might, power, and thought and his very own person and likeness, without giving praise or **(411v)** glory to God for the many gifts that God had given him.

And so the wrath of God came upon him and his descendants and his people in the way that Merlin said in his prophecy, because it was within himself that he brought about the vengeance, so that all the wealthy were punished, because the growth of every land failed. And yet despite his worldly fortune, he was unable to either overcome the Saxon peoples or drive them out of the island, as some of the authors have written. And one can imagine that all he wanted to do was win victories over his enemies in towns and on the battlefield and to make them subject to him ever more to satisfy his lust and greed for their goods and their land rather than settling them in good governance. The chronicles say that he intended to leave the people of the realm without governance and without a godly way of life. Some of them report that he was killed fighting in battle against his enemies, but some of the others say that God punished his body with disease, from which he died, as Guido and Geoffrey say, after he had been the king of this island for as long as forty-eight years.

CUSTENNIN AND THE RISE OF GWRTHEYRN/VORTIGERN

NLW MS 5276Dii

The name *Custennin* was latinized as *Constantine* by writers such as Bede and Geoffrey of Monmouth. His three sons were Constans (the Simple), Emrys Wledig, and Uthyr Pendragon. The name *Gwrtheyrn* was latinized as *Vortigern;* he is credited with having invited the Saxons to come to Britain to aid him in his many battles. Elis refers to the cadre of warriors that Gwrtheyrn hires to support him as "painted" people. The Romans called the Picts *picti,* supposedly meaning "painted people," but this etymology has no modern support.

(288r) Around this time [AD 433], Custennin was crowned the king of this island. He began to reform the temples and sent men to preach the Catholic faith among the Britons. Because of this he was called Custennin Fendigaid, "the Blessed." The stories about him tell that he had three sons from his queen shortly after they married. The first was Constans, who was simpleminded, and for that reason he was made a monk in a temple in Caerwynt that was called an undignified temple or a temple for the foolish. The other two were Emrys and Uthyr.

Now, at this time there was an adviser to the king and duke and ruler of a people who were called Jesses, who inhabited the land that lies east of Caer Ludd, which today is called Essex. This man, as the story says, was called in Welsh Gwrtheyrn and in English Vortigern. The story says that he was a man of much deceit and jealousy and very desirous of worldly riches and power and lordship over people. And so he planned night and day within himself how he might secretly **(288v)** betray the king so that he could gain the crown and rule the kingdom without anyone doubting or suspecting him. In the end, after long consultation with his deceitful friends, he arranged for one of his servants to be dressed as an envoy from a foreign land and sent with letters to the king. As the story relates, the king was staying in Caerwynt, and the traitor hastened there. He was brought before the king, who, as some of the stories relate, was in a private room. There, the story says, the traitor said he had certain matters to reveal to the king in private. Thereupon, the king ordered everyone out of the chamber, although other sources say that the king left his chamber and went outside to a secret garden to converse with the evil man. But indeed, it doesn't matter in which of the two places he was, either in the chamber or in the garden, because all of the authors agree that the man got the king alone and without any of the king's own men. The wretch immediately drew his hidden dagger and with it stabbed the king under his breast, twisting his body to observe him. From that wound the king died, having ruled as the king of this realm for ten years. The treacherous hand escaped untouched before any of the king's attendants thought that he was even half finished with his business.

News of the deed spread all across the country, to nobles and commoners, all of whom felt **(289r)** great sorrow over him, as they were called upon to do—and especially the courtiers, because of the indifference with which they greeted his death. And so, as soon as the bishop of Caer Ludd got word of what happened to the king, as we have recounted just now, he supposed that it was some of the king's council and the powerful ones of the realm who were guilty of that deed. So he took the two youngest sons of the king, Emrys and Uthyr, and sent them across the sea to Little Britain, for it was with him that the two boys were being taught and nurtured, as my author says. Also, he and most of the leaders of the realm supposed that Gwrtheyrn was guilty of the death of the king, which was true. But anyway, he had done this deed so secretly and so deviously that no one could prove anything against him as a conspirator in this act. To hide his evil plotting and his wickedness, he told his council that it was appropriate now for them to take Constans out of the temple for the foolish and make him the king of the realm. Some of his council agreed readily, but others did not consent, for they could see clearly that he was not fit to carry out the responsibilities of a king, owing to his lack of sense and wisdom. Nevertheless, Gwrtheyrn went to the temple where Constans was a monk performing religious rites and told him briefly what had happened to his father and how he was next in line to be the king and then arranged for him to leave the religious life in order to take over the rule of the realm. This would be much more appropriate and more fitting for him because of his birth and nature than remaining in the habit of a monk. Constans replied by saying, "Gwrtheyrn, you have to know that from my (289v) childhood until now I have learned nothing but praying to God, and so I am unable to understand anything of the way and manner for a man to perform in words and deeds to take up royal leadership upon himself to accomplish the rule of a realm and to defend it against sundry physical assaults." And when he had said that, Gwrtheyrn said as follows: "Constans, you must realize that you can gain God's blessing doing your work in ruling the people of your realm in peace and tranquillity as well as here in the garb of a man of religion." Constans replied and said, "Gwrtheyrn, you know full well that I haven't the sense to give answers to nobility and commoners." Gwrtheyrn answered this, saying, "You don't have to worry about the needs of the realm, for I will appoint councilors for you from among the wisest and most learned as can be found within the entire realm to deal with the concerns and needs of the governance of the kingdom, so that you will not have any more worry then than you have today."

In the end, with the flattery and urgency of Gwrthryrn, Constans left his monastery, gave up his pious ways and his monastic garb, and went with Gwrtheyrn. As some of the books say, he set many nobles of the realm whom he loved, as the Welsh proverb says, to hold to the same path as him, to crown Constans the king of Great Britain. As Geoffrey says, Constans was crowned the king of this island.

Following Custennin the Blessed, Constans his son was crowned king through the sophistry and urging of Gwrtheyrn and the support of most of the nobles of the realm in the year of the age of Christ 444. And as my author says, it was not long after the coronation of Constans (290r) before he put all the ruling of the realm into the possession and administration of Gwrtheyrn, to make and remake every single thing as it suited him. Gwrtheyrn took up all of this gladly. To bring about his ideas and intentions, in true cunning he secretly sent messengers to find as many as two hundred of the strongest, youngest, and most accomplished knights that could be found among the painted people to come to him. They came to him gladly. He pronounced them sworn followers and protectors of the king's person, for he knew perfectly well the nature of these people, who, as the authors say, were a poisonous, volatile people who lusted after minted coin, for which they would mercilessly do any misdeed. The chief or captain of these men was Gwrtheyrn, who gave them plenty, including gifts of gold and silver and clothing, making them different by far from any of the knights of the kingdom, intending that somehow through their deeds they would kill the king in some mysterious way, by telling these evil men while giving them gifts words like "Men, if I were king of this realm, I would make much more of you than is being done now." It was words such as these that emboldened the false knights to plot treachery against the king, saying among themselves, "It's a shame for us to allow and suffer this mere shadow to live and keep such a fine and praiseworthy person as Gwrtheyrn (290v) from the crown. 'Tis better for him to be the king than this shadow of a man with neither thought, memory, or sense to know who was serving him well and who was not." They also said among themselves, "Without a doubt, there is no one on this island more worthy of wearing the crown than Gwrtheyrn if Constans's head were off his body." And after these evil men consulted together about the matter, they agreed to kill the king. So that night they went to the king in his chambers, where they murdered him by cutting off his head. And that is how he died, a simple martyr, having worn the crown for four years.

These accursed men sent the head as a present to the captain, asking him to rejoice and take up the rule of the kingdom and be king. But with cunning, as soon as he saw the head, the story says that he feigned grief and great sorrow over his death. And yet the story shows that he had never been happier in his heart. Some of the writers say that he wept waters from his eyes, more from joy over the death of the king and to hide his wickedness so he could win the goodwill of some of the Britons who suspected him in the death of Custennin. Because of that he had the evil knights seized suddenly and put into a secure prison in the city of Caer Ludd, where eventually he had them all cruelly put to death, as if he himself considered that the deed they had (291r) done was extremely grievous. And so the Britons understood that Gwrtheyrn was innocent of all the sins they had accused him of. And not long afterward the leaders of the realm agreed to make him the king.

GWRTHEYRN AND SAINT GERMAIN

NLW MS 5276Dii

Germain (380–c. 448) was the bishop of Auxerre when he was urged to go to Britain around 430 with Lupus of Troyes to combat Pelagianism.

He later made a second trip to Britain in the company of Severus, the bishop of Trèves.

(294r) At that time, as the two learned authors Phillipus and Antonius write, two holy men came from Gaul to preach the Catholic faith among the Britons and the Saxons. They were called Saints Germain and Lupus. The two authors say that the two holy men arrived near the court of Gwrtheyrn when he was hunting in the country. They (294v) stopped in a village where there were few beds. Because the holy man was not able to find lodging, he walked on until he was beside the king's court. The king encountered Saint Germain, as the two authors mentioned above relate, who asked the king to get some of his servants to find them a place to sleep in a bed in the town or village near the court. The king abruptly refused, so the holy man and his companion took their rest under the branches in a thicket. It happened that one of the men who cared for some of the king's animals found them arranging a place to lie down and pass the night. He felt pity and mercy for the situation of Germain and his companion and brought them to his house. Then and there, he slaughtered and dressed the only calf he owned, to give comfort and welcome to the bishop and his companion. Afterward, the holy bishop instructed the man to gather all the calf's bones and put them in the stall in front of the cow. The man and his wife did that gladly and obediently. Then, the next morning, they found the calf alive. Then, as the legend and life of Bishop Germain Vincent recount, he asked the hospitable man to come with him to the king's court, which the herdsman happily did. There the bishop had a conversation with the king, in which he asked him why his heart was so hard that he could, in his heart, refuse him lodging. The king did not answer. Then the holy man said, "In the name of the highest Lord, the one eternal God, I order you to go away (295r) and vanish now and leave your court and your kingship to this herdsman, who is more worthy to hold the royal rule than you." As the legend of the bishop reveals, Gwrtheyrn did that at once, through the power of God. In his place, Germain made the herdsman king. This was in the year of the age of Christ 451 and in the second year of the reign of Clodion, the king of the Franks.

Although this text takes its authority from a holy and saintly man, it still depicts more of wonder than of reality. Also, other writings say that it was with a man called Bule, the king of Powys, that this story happened with Saint Germain. And since the bishop does not give the name of the herdsman, the man the story says was made king, it's likely that the whole story is fictitious, for his life says that he went to France right after he unseated Gwrtheyrn, which is unlikely to be true, because there wasn't any bishop for baptized Christians in France at that time, nor for faithful believers, as the author Jacobus Renensis says. He was one of the men who brought the Franks to the faith in the year of the age of Christ 499. That was in the fifteenth year of the reign of Clodovius, the king of the Franks.

GWRTHEYRN AND THE FALLING CASTLE

NLW MS 5276Dii

This story marks the epiphany of Merlin, whose arrival into the world is told in "The Birth of Merlin the Prophet." Gwrtheyrn's wise men, who are at a loss to explain the falling castle, make up the story of the boy born without a father, which, of course, turns out to be true. Naturally, they encounter Merlin in the city of Caerfyrddin (modern Carmarthen), whose name the early, folk etymology assumed meant "Myrddin's fortified town [*caer*]." While Elis doesn't necessarily believe in Merlin's prophecies here, he holds that reading such material is at least better than idleness, in that it encourages reflection and sharpens the intellect.

(303v) At this time, the story says that Gwrtheyrn asked for advice from his closest advisers about what was the best thing he could plan and do to protect against the cruelty of the hated enemy. These advisers were mostly British nobles, who, after some discussion, advised him to build a castle in that place to defend against the enemy. And so he set people to work immediately on an open ground or clearing of land, where the diggers will encounter an obstacle, as this work will soon show. In that place, the stonemasons had the foundation dug and the base for the wall all around the site and began to raise the wall to a certain height above the ground. The story says that as much as they raised during the day would fall at night. Because of that, as my author writes, Gwrtheyrn and his wise men were struck dumb. And so he summoned as many philosophers, necromancers, and sorcerers of the arts as he could find throughout the realm, men to whom ordinary people gave their greatest trust, in order to find out through these arts and skilled people **(304r)** what it was that caused the work to fall at night rather than in the day. But anyway, after each of them had tried their arts and skills to find the reason why the work was falling, not one of them could find a single natural cause why the work was falling at night and not in the day. But each of them told his opinion, what he thought, and his conjecture, all of which was far from the real reason—this they knew. And yet the common people, forgiving the wise ones, believed firmly that there was nothing that was unknown to them. And so to blind and beguile Gwrtheyrn and his council, they told him that the work would never stand until they had found a son without a father, killed him, and taken his blood and mixed it with the mortar. The work would stand safe thenceforth.

And as the opinion of the learned ones makes clear, they didn't say any of these words because every one of them knew that such a boy, a boy without a father, could never be found, because they understood that the begetting and birth of such a child was against reason and nature. And so they were certain and believed firmly that there was no way to find such a child. Nevertheless, it wasn't long before Gwrtheyrn sent messengers with letters far and near, as far as the sea and nearby, asking about such a child who had no father. And then, after much searching, one of the messengers came to a town in south Wales that is now called Caerfyrddin, where, as the story recounts, the messenger heard two young boys reviling each other. In anger and spite, one of them said to the other, "It is a shame to have to ask and seek to know who your father **(304v)** is." Whereupon the other said something like "As for my father, it matters not to you what or who my father is, for I have enough sense and intelligence to provide answers to your foolishness." The other answered and said, "It is very true, Merlin, and I confess that I do not have either sense or intelligence or reason or knowledge such as you have. But despite that, most people say truly that your intelligence and knowledge do not come from God, the Father of all powers, because none of the people know who your father is, though many people know your mother."

Well, as soon as the messenger heard these or similar words, he and the others who were involved in the search carefully asked the neighbors about where and from what people Merlin had come. They told him in some detail the whole story of that which has been told earlier in this work. And as soon as the messengers heard the whole story, they sought out the nobles and rulers of the city and Aldan until the rulers were willing to allow Merlin and his mother to go with them and agree that it was proper for them to go. In haste, the messengers led the mother and son before Gwrtheyrn, who, as the story says, welcomed them warmly, and especially Aldan, whom he and his council questioned privately to seek the truth about how she became pregnant with the boy. She, the story shows, told the king the story discussed earlier, through her tears, from beginning to end.

When Gwrtheyrn had heard it all in detail, he stood astonished and looked at Merlin, who was present there. Then, the story continues, Merlin spoke to Gwrtheyrn and told him, "Don't be too vexed or overcome with wonder at the words my mother has spoken, for you don't need any more information in this matter than you have already been told just now. **(305r)** I am asking and entreating you to show me why Your Grace had me and my mother brought here from my birthplace to this place." The story says that the king explained the entire matter to him in detail, and when Merlin had understood it, he said this to the king: "Certainly, it is in your power and your authority to do as you please, either killing me or not, but I say to Your Grace that the wall will not stand just because you mix my blood with the mortar, for it is unlikely that one can raise the wall even a hand's height with what mortar can be made with my blood. And as for the plan, your structure is ill conceived." Gwrtheyrn responded and said, "Understand that it was not my idea to order your death but that of my sorcerers, who told me that the wall would not stand except for your death." At that, Merlin asked the king to summon the diviners before him, which the king was pleased to do. All these wise men and those learned in all the arts were brought before the king. It was a huge gathering of people. There, as the story shows, Merlin asked in the presence of the crowd why they saw that the structure could stand only with his death. They answered after some discussion that they did not see any remedy in their arts to make the wall stand except with the blood of a boy who had no father. Whereupon Merlin said, "O you untruthful, lying people, your reason is far from the true cause for the work's falling." The outburst stunned the wise ones. And then Merlin said to the king, "Gwrtheyrn, Your Grace must now know clearly that under the foundation of the wall there lies something that prevents the wall from standing." The king asked him what it was that made the wall fall. Merlin spoke at length as follows:

"Sire, under the stone foundation there lies a lake of still water. In it there reside two vicious creatures who since long ago have created much havoc and discord, and for that they have been buried and hidden in this lake. Their natures and temperaments are at odds with each (305v) other, so that they fight twice every twenty-four hours. From the struggle and turmoil of these dragons fighting in the enclosed body of water, the earth shakes, and this is what makes your wall fall down."

Gwrtheyrn set his people to work digging into the earth to find the lake, which they did quickly. The story goes on to say that with much labor and cost, trenches and ditches were made to drain the lake and make it dry so they could examine it. And after draining the water from the lake, they found two dragons, just as Merlin had said. The story says that one of them was red and the other white. As soon as they were awakened from their sleep, they turned upon each other to fight and a fierce battle ensued, witnessed by the entire assemblage. In the struggle, the red dragon retreated from the middle of the lake to the far edge, whereupon, as my source says, Merlin bowed his head and in sadness wept a tear. And in a moment they fought a second battle in the same way. In this battle the red dragon was defeated, taking to her wings and flying from one corner of the spot where the lake had been to the other. And in the end she opened her wings to take flight and fly away. As the authors tell it, when she took flight, the red dragon broke the tail of the white one as she rose. Thereupon each withdrew from the other: one flew toward the east and the other toward the west. Gwrtheyrn and his people marveled greatly at that, so much so that the king asked Merlin many questions about what the dragons and their battles signified. Merlin replied, saying as follows:

(306r) "Gwrtheyrn, the two dragons you saw here just now represent the two races of men, whose customs and natures are as incompatible and contentious as the temperaments of the two dragons you saw fighting in this watery place. Of these, the red dragon represents and signifies the race of the Britons, and the white one represents the Saxon nations to whom you gave permission and welcomed to stay and dwell on this island, for which you and your court are now very sorry for having done. And just as you saw the white dragon overcome the red one in fighting, so the race of Saxons overcame and will overcome the Britons, whom they will drive from the fertile lands of the realm to the wilderness, just as you saw the red dragon flee to the far edge of the watery place. But in the end the Britons will overcome the foreign race, for in the same way that you saw the red dragon winning in the end and cutting off the tail of the white one as she flew off, so the Britons will conquer in the end by cutting the foreigners' tails short in the last battle, so that they won't be carrying even a stick from that time on and will have no power within this realm."

As Geoffrey's story shows, Merlin then made prophecies as he sat at the edge of the watery place. In the opinion of a number of people in the world from that time to this, these reveal all of every sort of conflict, pleasure, and progress that ever was and will be on this island forever. There have been and still are some credulous Britons who have put their complete trust in these. But learned scholars have no faith in them at all or in the sort of stubborn, difficult Briton who sees these as true, and they scorn the great man. And yet the sayings reproduced here exist among the Britons in writing and are widespread among the people in (306v) Welsh and among the English in Latin and English. But there is not much authority to show that everything therein is true. And yet by the Blessed God who ordained everything that has been and will be, I am not able to feel or see that there is any harm coming out of it or developing from it for anyone who may read it or any such things as may be seemly to read. And indeed, I can see that for anyone who takes the trouble to read such matter as this, there are three things that profit both body and soul. The first is that it is sure and certain that he will not be idle while reading such material. The second advantage is that a benefit comes to such a person who reads it because from steady reading and careful thinking comes reflection and understanding, which hones and sharpens the intellect to be ready to smoothly chisel away at similes and obscure and dark proverbs so that it is easier for others to understand them. And the third advantage is that whoever may read them seriously, calling upon God for help in understanding them, will receive understanding of various things that have passed and knowledge of such things as may be likely to occur, along with the three corporal benefits of passing the time, fighting idleness, and practicing discourse.

The story also says that Merlin asked Gwrtheyrn to leave the work standing and find a place to defend himself from the cruelty of the sons of Custennin, who were preparing a fleet to bring soldiers to avenge the blood of their father and brother on him.

GWRTHEYRN'S REIGN, HENGIST, AND HORSA

NLW MS 5276Dii

This story recounts a critical episode in the early history of Britain, the advent of the Saxons to the island and the welcome and lofty positions given to the leaders and their lieutenants. Elis spells Hengist's name as *Engiest,* indicating that the *g* should be pronounced as *j*. Both *Hengist* and *Horsa* are words for "horse," though the former may refer to a gelding.

(291r) At this time, 465 AD, as Fabyan says, God sent death from a plague within this realm that was so severe that the living could scarcely bury the dead. The *Polychronicon* says that from weariness and fear and grief, Gwrtheyrn sent messengers to the Saxons to try to get some people **(291v)** to help and support him against the Picts, who were daily threatening to invade. This, as my source shows, was in the year of the age of Christ 451, which was in the third year of the reign of Gwrtheyrn. At this time, three long ships landed in the realm and country now called Kent, full of young men in harness. Some of the books say that these men had been sent to help him, but Geoffrey says that they landed in that place by accident and from there they were eventually brought to the king. Their captains were two men, one called Horn or Horsus and the other Engiest. These two were brought before the king, who asked them through an interpreter what path or route they had taken to this island and what people they came from. Engiest replied, saying they were descended from the line of Estressimius son of Noah, as will be shown further on in the present work, in the way that certain lineages went into the realms of Germania, whence he and his people came.

After a long discussion, the king asked him why they had come away from the land of their birth in that way. Engiest answered, saying, "The custom among the princes of the country we come from is, when the number of persons within the realms exceeds the fruits of labor, to pick and choose from among the youths of the realm the strongest and sturdiest and best trained. These they prepare and train at the expense of the nobles and commons of the **(292r)** realm so that they can earn their livelihood by volunteering their bodies in battles or other ventures in the service of a chieftain or king. And that is how on this occasion we agreed to leave the land of our birth in three boats, in which, through the power of the gods, we came across the deep ocean to land in this realm." The king asked Engiest what god he and his people believed in. He replied that of the gods it was the sun and the moon that they believed in chiefly, and after that each of the rest of the planets in order. The story says that after more conversation, the king said these words or something similar: "Sirs, whatever need or circumstance caused you to leave your country and has brought you to the shore of this realm, I welcome each and every one of you, for I need the help of men of war." And he immediately took them into his service gladly, for at the time the Picts were beginning to enter the realm in various places. With these new soldiers, Gwrtheyrn confronted the Picts, and in mighty battles he achieved victory over the painted ones. The story shows that then and there the Saxons did their part as brave and mighty men.

And so Gwrtheyrn took all of the pagans into his court to be closest to him, sworn to protect him. But despite all of this, Saint Bede, who wrote the .*Ecclesiastical History of the* (292v) *English People* in the year of Christ 730 doesn't mention a single word about Custennin the Blessed coming from Little Britain, nor about his three sons, Constans, Emrys, and Uthyr, and yet he wrote about the time and rule of Gwrtheyrn in detail and how he sent messengers to find Saxons to help him against his enemies. Geoffrey agrees with this, saying that King Gwrtheyrn often took as many as eleven hundred Saxons as men sworn to him. Because of that, the Britons became angry at the king, for taking so many pagans at once into his service and for including them in the realm. But their anger and displeasure did not change the king's will and affection for the foreigners. And because of his affection for them, he did much more for them than he did for any of his own men of the realm, and so jealously gradually brought disunity and wrath until there was exceeding hatred between the Britons and the Saxons. This resulted in many casualties on both sides, and so Engiest complained bitterly against the Britons to the king, pleading with him about having a place and spot to build a stronghold such as a castle or town to keep themselves together and away from the cruelty and anger and ferocity of the Britons, who were destroying them daily, as wolves destroy sheep. But it was not easy for the king to allow any of the pagans' requests and petitions, for all the nobles of the Britons were greatly against them. (293r) Engiest saw this readily and eventually asked the king and his council to grant him an amount of land within the kingdom that could be encircled with a single strip of animal hide. This the king allowed. Engiest took the largest animal he could find and had its skin cut off. This he cut around in a single tiny strip and with it encircled a section of land in which he then built a castle, which is now called Thong Castle or Castle of the Leather Strips. Engiest had it built in great haste and under pressure.

However, there exist differing accounts in the chronicles. Some of the writers say that it was in the land called Kent that he built this castle, and the men of Kent say that the remains of the ditches and buildings still stand beside the town of Sittingbourne and that the place retains the name Thong Castle. Other books say that it was in the land which was called Caer Llwydcoed and is now Lincolnshire. But wherever the remains of this castle stand, it has to lie on the shore of a branch of the sea, because Geoffrey says that Engiest sent some messengers across the sea to ask his peoples to secretly send him some of the wisest, most intelligent, and most ardent soldiers to protect and defend the castle. He asked them to send certain provisions and his two sons, Octa and Offa, and his daughter, Rhonwen. Eventually, all of this came across the sea to Engiest's castle, **(293v)** secretly and without the king's knowledge. But some of the chronicles say that as many as a hundred ships crossed the sea to him at that time, and this seems to be true. But anyway, as soon as the castle was completed and full of every necessity, as Geoffrey shows, Engiest prepared a huge feast, to which he invited the king. The king accepted, and the story says that the king was given a great welcome and many gifts.

As the king was leaving the feast to take the evening's rest, as is natural for every creature since God put flesh and bone together, at that moment, as Geoffrey writes, Engiest's daughter, Rhonwen, came and knelt before the king with a gold cup full of hippocras. With carefully chosen words, she offered the drink to the king, saying "Wasael." This was likely on the eve of the feast of the Epiphany in the Christmas season, because this word was and is usual among the Saxons in various places within the realm. As soon as the king understood through the translator what she had said, the king answered in the same language, "Trynk hael"—that is, "Drink in health." And as the story goes, a spark of love for Rhonwen was struck in the king's heart because of her face, her bearing, and her decorum. A short time afterward, he married her, for he was a widower at the time. All the authors agree that at the wedding and the wedding feast, (294r) Gwrtheyrn gave all the land around the castle to Engiest and to his brother and to their people to dwell and remain in. This soon caused great sorrow among the Britons, because the king began to grow more negligent and careless about keeping law and justice between the weak and the strong. And he did not much care about what sort of disorder and unruliness existed between nobles and commoners of the realm if it suited his new allies in keeping the peace. This made the Britons hostile and filled with malice toward the king and his new kindred. In the same way, these new kindred were hostile to the Britons and feared them greatly, just as the Britons feared the Saxons, and with reason, for the Saxons were increasing greatly in numbers. And so, after much secret discussion of the matter, the Britons put their heads together to take counsel about what they could devise and do against the negligence of the king and the rapacity and wickedness of the Saxons, and also against the king's lack of faith, which was the opinion of the Sectarians.

[The story of Gwrtheyrn and Saint Germain is inserted at this point; see above.]

(295r) A short time after this, as the previous authors show, a great number of ships full of people came across the sea from Saxon lands. They all came ashore on this island. They were all descended from three groups, Saxons, Nichtys[?], and Angles. They will be discussed here in this (295v) work further on when the time comes. For now, I will turn to the work of Geoffrey, who, as this work has shown previously, has told how the Britons went to council to destroy the arrogance of the Saxons. At the time, after long discussion they could see that there was no way for them to bring about their goals other than to remove Gwrtheyrn from his royal rule. This they did immediately, taking him and imprisoning him without most of his servants knowing. This happened, as many of the books say, in the sixth year of his reign. Others say that it was in the tenth year of his reign that he was brought down from his supremacy. But it doesn't matter which of the two is correct, for they all agree that he was brought down and that Vortimer his son was made the king. . . .

(297r) In the end, the Britons deprived Gwrtheyrn of the privileges of kingship and exiled him from the realm, according to some of the writers, but others say that they put him in prison. But indeed, it doesn't matter which of those two the Britons did with him, because all of the authors agree that they removed the king from the throne and crowned Vortimer, or, as some of the books call him, Gwrthefyr, Gwrtheyrn's son by his first wife as the king of this island in the **(297v)** year of the age of Christ 464. As Geoffrey shows, Gwrthefyr had the Britons mobilize soldiers in several places of the realm shortly after being crowned king. He goes on to write that with these forces, Gwrthefyr attacked the Saxons in four severe and merciless battles. The first of these was within Kent, where Engiest was the lord, on the shore of the river called Arwent, where the Britons were victorious. The second battle against the Saxons was on the banks of the water and ford known at the time as Ippsford or Sliford in the land now called Norfolk and beside the town now known as Thetford. From there the pagans retreated toward Kent. Some of the books say that at that time Catageni the king's brother encountered Horsus, Engiest's brother. But other books say that he was just one of the Britons' captains. But it doesn't matter which it was, because they met on a bridge over a river that flows through the town that lies between Caer Goel and Caer Ludd in the land now known as Essex and the town of Chaunceford, where the story says they were all killed in the battle. Some were killed defending the bridge and the others trying to conquer it. That was the third battle.

(298r) After this, the Britons relentlessly pursued the Saxons day and night, forcing them all to flee to the island that lies in the eastern part of Kent, now known as Dënned Island. That is where the fourth battle took place, where, as Geoffrey writes, the Britons got the upper hand through God's miracle and the prayers of Bishop Germain Vincent, who was among the Britons at the time. The fighting was so fierce that the Britons turned from the enemy, thinking to flee, but the holy bishop turned his face to the sky and cried out, "Alleluia, alleluia." Upon hearing those words, the Britons turned back to the enemy with courage and slew many of them. King Gwrthefyr gave permission to Engiest and the living who were able to travel to leave the land. Some of the wounded Saxons who were baptized were given permission to remain in the land. One of these was Rhonwen daughter of Engiest. She was angry and regretful about the fall of her husband the king and the slaughter of her people and their exile from the land. Because of that she summoned all her mortal powers to change her situation. To make that happen, she needed to get her husband out of prison, but she could see that this would be impossible to achieve while Gwrthefyr (or Vortimer) was alive, for he was much loved by the Britons. So she decided to poison him. She could not accomplish this without the help of some of his attendants and did not rest night or day to accomplish her wicked plan. In the end, she came to know an evil man, one of the king's chamberlains, to whom she gave and promised more immeasurable amounts of money to poison his master. This he did, eager from lust for her monies, and that is how Gwrthefyr died of poison in the seventh year of his reign. His death was greatly mourned by the Britons, as it was their nature to do.

MERLIN AND STONEHENGE

NLW MS 5276Dii

According to Geoffrey of Monmouth, Emrys (Ambrosius Aurelianus) was the son of Custennin (Constantine) and brother of Uthyr Pendragon and therefore an uncle of Arthur's. Caer Ludd is the Welsh name for London; Elis occasionally uses the English name or the Welsh one, Lloegr. The opening line of this tale refers to Emrys's victory over the Anglo-Saxons. Elis's doubt about the story of the stones focuses not on Merlin's wisdom but on Elis's own scientific analysis. The reference to Stonehenge and its location on the Salisbury Plain is clear.

(316r) After Emrys brought peace to this island and destroyed the rule of law of the paynims and subdued them to his rule and restored and repaired the temples and churches, he asked the bishop of Caer Ludd, the king and his council, to create some splendid works at the place where the Saxons slew the princes of the realm so that there would be remembrance of the shame of the encounter and of their deaths. For advice in the matter, the king and his court sought out Merlin, who was found in Glyn Galabes, whence he was brought before the king, who asked his advice. When he had heard what the king and his court wanted, Merlin said as follows: "Indeed, there are certain stones or large rocks atop a high mountain that the giants of Ireland brought and carried from distant lands and placed there for their numerous qualities. With all of the properties these stones had, the giants healed every sort of wound and injury and sickness, by means of people either getting water from the stones or coming and rubbing their bodies against the stones."

There was much conversation and discussion, with the king and his court mocking Merlin for (316v) saying that the rocks or stones from Ireland were better that the big stones of Britain. Nevertheless, as soon as the king and his court heard Merlin discussing the unique qualities and virtues of the stones, they agreed to make ships ready and assembled soldiers, over whom King Emrys made Uthyr his brother the chieftain or captain. When the soldiers had boarded the ship, he had the sailors lift anchors and raise sails, and immediately they took to the sea toward Ireland. Uthyr and his men reached land near the tallest mountain, to which, on Merlin's advice, Uthyr quickly led his men. There, as the story says, the Britons wondered greatly at the way the stones had been made to stand and at their size. Then Merlin brought together all the young men to test their fortitude, ability, and strength, to pull down the stones and drag them to the ships. But as the story goes, after all the young ones tested their ability and their strength, Merlin clearly demonstrated that the cunning of art is stronger than human strength and might alone, and so with Merlin's wisdom and art he soon brought these stones to the shore. But as the rest of the story shows, before they could be loaded on the ships, word came to the Irish king, Gwilmor, that strangers, foreigners, were taking the tall, narrow stones out of the island. He mustered some men, and with these he waged battle against Uthyr. On this field, many Irish were killed, so the king had to retreat and muster more men. By that time, the Britons had loaded the ships with the stones and boarded their ships. And by the time that Gwilmor and his (317r) men returned, the Britons were aboard their boats and sailing back to this island, where they arrived safely.

A while later they took the rocks to the mound or prominence where the nobles mentioned earlier had been killed and buried, and there these rocks were set, according to Merlin's instructions, in an excellent arrangement and formation. And truly, their arrangement is amazing and their size such that whoever might journey past this open field beside the town now called Salisbury can see them.

But despite all that, the learned ones do not agree with any of the sense of this story, for they hold strongly to the notion that none of these stones were brought from Ireland through the advice and cunning of Merlin, as Geoffrey says. Rather, the learned and knowing men say that the making of these stones was done from limestone burned by flint and cement and poured into a mold and then baked, as is done with various stones today in various ways. This seems likely to be true, because all but two of the stones are of the same shape, form, and size. And these two stones, one smaller than the other, are of the same thickness. And this is also similar to the opinion of the scholars, because only rarely and seldom does one get stones of the same size as these out of a quarry. Furthermore, if we could raise stones from a quarry or quarries that were the size of these again, we would only rarely see stones quarried from a rock of the same color throughout in every stone, like these stones—and of the same hardness everywhere, for they are so hard that there are no steel or iron tools that can hew any of them. And all their gritty surfaces are of the same kind and color and the surface dust of the same thickness. And for these reasons and **(317v)** many others, the men of learning say with conviction that they were made in a mold, as said earlier, from lime and cement.

MERLIN EXPLAINS THE DRAGON IMAGE

NLW MS 5276Dii

Uthyr's epithet, Pendragon, may literally mean "head of a dragon," but as it occurs in some of the earliest bardic poetry addressed to a chieftain, it rather means "head" or "chief" dragon, a term reserved for a leader. Elis, apparently following Geoffrey of Monmouth here, takes the word literally and so has it breathing fires, whose meanings Merlin can interpret.

(317v) At this time, Emrys had fallen ill and was lying in Caerwynt. **(318r)** That is why the king was unable to be physically present in the field to encounter his enemies. The council agreed to transfer authority to his brother Uthyr, who quickly assembled soldiers and prepared them for battle. He led them to the place where Pasgen and Gwilmor were preparing to depart the country, even though they were calling themselves heirs of the land. But as the story goes, Pasgen and Gwilmor realized that they would never be able to achieve their goals while Emrys, whom the nobles and commoners of the realm loved, was still alive. They heard that he was lying ill in Caerwynt. Pasgen began to give careful consideration to how he could kill and destroy Emrys secretly and deceitfully. He shared his thoughts with the king of Ireland and all of his fellow conspirators. One of these was a Saxon named Klappa Korppa or Ioppa. This one took it upon himself to kill Emrys before he could return to his people. He left the council at once, disguised himself, and changed his clothing and dressed himself in physician's garb. He set off accompanied by some assistants of the art and came to Caerwynt. There he made a proclamation in the town's marketplace, made signs, and put them up on posts at street corners, announcing to all the townspeople that such physicians had come to the town. He pretended that he made men and women well from many kinds of ailments and diseases. As a result, he was brought in confidence to the king, to whom, as the story reveals, he gave a drink to make him sleep. Klappa then quickly took to horse. **(318v)** Shortly thereafter, the king died, in Caerwynt, having ruled, according to most of the authorities, as long as nineteen years.

On the second day after his death, as my source says, which accords with the body of the story, in the early hours of the morning there appeared a star in the firmament which, the story says, glowed as brightly as the sun. On one side of it there appeared the semblance of a dragon, his mouth open, from which shot out two brilliant shafts of light, burning like fiery flames glowing brightly. One of these shafts stretched toward Gaul. This, as Geoffrey's account says, grew or moved toward seven shafts or seven beams of light, burning like flames of fire. The other shaft or beam stretched toward Ireland, and it too was a fiery flame. Everyone looked long and marveled at the magnificent display there in the firmament. Afterward, as the story says clearly, Uthyr and the council of the realm had Merlin brought before them to hear his understanding and meaning of what the appearance of the star meant. Soon, this is what he told them:

"You must know that yonder star indicates wonder and sadness. First of all, it shows that King Emrys has died of poison. The dragon's head signifies Uthyr, who is here present. He will be the king of this realm. The shaft that stretches from the head of the dragon to the south means that Uthyr will have a son who will overcome and conquer all the realms of Gaul and France. And he will be the most highly praised and of the greatest honor that there has ever been or ever will be on this island. And the seven shafts show that under him there will be seven strong kings. **(319r)** The shaft that stretches toward the west indicates that Uthyr will have a daughter who will be the queen of Ireland, from whom will spring many noble chieftains."

Following this, as the story says, Merlin asked Uthyr to regroup the men and go boldly against the enemy. This they did the following morning. And on this occasion, after long fighting, Uthyr and his brave men got the upper hand over their enemies, Uthyr killing Pasgen and Gwilmor with his own hand. But some of the authors say that he killed only Pasgen and that the king of Ireland fled with a number of his people. Some of the Britons happened to meet them fleeing toward their ships and attacked them mercilessly. Gwilmor and his entire family were killed there. After that, the Britons seized the enemy ships. Following their victory, Uthyr and the nobles of the realm went to Caerwynt, where they conducted the funeral for King Emrys. The Britons of the court had Emrys buried among the pillars, among the bones of the nobles, where Merlin had set the stones. From that time and long after, the place was called Cerrigle, "the place of the rocks," and that's where many of the leaders of this island were buried long afterward.

UTHYR DEFEATS THE SAXONS, ARTHUR IS BORN

NLW MS 5276Dii

The story of the birth of Arthur is yet another birth tale motivated by lust and passion and enabled by magic. Like the story of the birth of Hercules (see part 1), it involves magic and shape-shifting and an eternal triangle: with Hercules, it is Jupiter, Amphitryon, and Alcmene; here, Uthyr, Gorlois, and Eigr. It is the rapacious lust of Uthyr that compels him to insult an important guest at his great feast held to celebrate his victories over the Saxons on the feast of Whitsuntide. When Uthyr can't take his eyes and his desire off Eigr, her husband, Gwrlois or Gorlois, takes her and his entourage and departs without permission from the king. Uthyr then pursues him and, thanks to Merlin's magic, sleeps with Eigr. She claims that the resulting pregnancy is due to her husband, but Uthyr calculates the timing and knows that the child is his. Merlin supplies the name Arthur for the child, who, again on Merlin's advice, is raised in fosterage by a nobleman living at Llyn Tegid. Perhaps not coincidentally, the story of Gwion Bach, who is reborn as

Taliesin, is set at the home of a nobleman who lived at Llyn Tegid and had a wife, Ceridwen, who was skilled in the arts of magic, enchantment, and divination (see part 3).

(320v) When Uthyr defeated the Saxons, most of the foreigners were killed. Octa and Offa were seized and sent to a strong prison in London. Uthyr proceeded to York, where he gave permission to his soldiers to return to their homes, leaving certain of his nobles and commoners (321r) to hold the land around York. Then he returned to Caer Ludd, where he wore his crown in honor the next Easter after that battle.

At that time, as Geoffrey has shown, the king proclaimed a triumph and games to be held on the next Whitsuntide. He invited all the chieftains of the land and their wives. And some of the authors have claimed that at the feast, the king provided a hundred thousand fatted oxen and as many various cattle and immeasurable quantities of different sorts of birds both wild and domestic. And some hold the opinion that this was the greatest of the three enormous feasts. By order of the king, the leaders of the realm came to the feast, as was fitting and proper. And when the day and time came, all the leaders and their wives came to the court. As the feast began, each of the nobles was placed to sit according to his lineage and his rank, and his wife beside him, as determined by the heralds. In time, the king took notice of the shape, aspect, composure, sensitivity, intelligence, beauty, and manner of Eigr, the wife of Gorlois, Earl of Cornwall. Love and desire for her kindled a flame of Venus's desire in the heart of the king such that he could not take his eyes off her. In time, the earl saw that the king had given his heart wholly to the lady. So the earl took his wife and a number of his retainers and departed suddenly for Cornwall without bidding farewell to the king, fearing that the king would spoil the chastity of his lady, angry and upset at the king's innuendo and affectionate conversation with his lady.

As soon as the king got word that the earl and his people had left the court in anger, he sent messengers to ask him to return to the court, and that at the cost of his head. But the earl did not comply with the king's request. The king became very angry, so angry at the earl that he proclaimed him a traitor disobedient to him and to the kingdom if he would not return (321v) to the court, he and his lady, by such and such a day. But the earl stood firm in his resolve, so firm that the king mustered some men for the purpose of making war against the earl, who had taken refuge in his castle, which, according to my author, was called Tintagel. The king made a formidable siege, so violent that one of the king's men asked why he was making full war against such a man who had done so much for him and given such service as Gorlois had given to him and to his brother. The king said it was because of the love and passion for Eigr that he was so angry at the earl, whom he had threatened to kill in order to have his way with Eigr, telling the knight his private thoughts and saying that if he could not get a moment's desire with Eigr he would go out of his mind and his senses. The knight told him to tell his secret to Merlin, which the king did without delay.

When Merlin heard the king's complaint, he asked the king to have soldiers ready to assault the castle at suppertime in the evening. On that occasion, Merlin, through his arts, would cast a spell over the king and Ulffios his chamberlain, whom he would make to look like the earl and his chamberlain, Jordan. And at the height of the assault between the two forces, Merlin would tell the the king to approach the gate of the castle directly and ask the porter to open the gate. This the king did quickly, and the keeper let in the king in the shape of his master the earl, who shortly before had been let out of the castle through a secret door so he could go out and fight his enemies, as he had often done in times when the king laid siege to his castle. And in this shape and form Uthyr entered the castle, and Merlin caused the king's men to halt the siege, in which Gorlois the earl was killed, and so Uthyr fulfilled his desire with Eigr, who, as my author shows, became pregnant by the king on this night.

(322r) On the following morning, the king went to his tents to his council, where word came that the earl had been killed during the assault that night. The news caused Eigr great sorrow and anger. But the story shows that Uthyr did not allow Eigr much time to grieve, because he quickly married her, and shortly after the wedding she knew she was pregnant, and this made her very sad, because, as the story goes, as she was carrying her burden she believed that Gorlois was the father of the child. Later, after much conversation, the king asked her why she was so sorrowful. She told him the source of her sorrow. But the king knew the time of night when the earl had been killed and the time when he lay with her. And so it was understood that the pregnancy was due to the king.

On the advice of Merlin, the child was named Arthur. Also, some of the books say that Merlin asked that this boy, a gift to the king, be reared in fosterage until he was of a certain age. After some deliberation, the king agreed. The one to whom the boy was given in fosterage was a respected nobleman named Cynnydd Gain Farfog, who dwelt beside Llyn Tegid in the land of Penllyn. His wife was one of the fairest and gentlest women in the land. She nurtured the boy at her breast.

Uthyr also had a daughter from Eigr. She was named Amia, and some of the books say that she married the king of Ireland, but others say that she married Lord Lyons. That could be true, because some of the French authors say that a great part of Galia was held by Uthyr Pendragon.

THE DEATH OF UTHYR PENDRAGON

NLW MS 5276Dii

Note that this story directly follows the preceding one, on 322r.

(322r) After King Uthyr had governed this realm benignly for a number of years, he fell ill with a disease. This was a great misfortune for the country, for at the time some emissaries from the Saxon countries had come to discuss getting Octa and Offa released from the prison where they had been held in Caer Ludd for a very long time, as the present work has previously shown. As the king was not willing to set them free upon payment of a sum of money, what the emissaries did was negotiate secretly with the men who guarded the place where Octa and Offa were being (322v) held. After some discussion, the guards agreed to release the pair for a certain sum of money. When they had been set free, the two fled across the sea to Germania. There, after some time, with effort and help from their people and kinsmen, they gathered a large host of soldiers and led them into the heart of this island. The Britons rose up against them, but because the Britons lacked a leader, the Saxons won the fortified town of Brilianus from them.

At that time, the royal authority was given to one of the king's close kinsmen, who, according to my copy, was called Dianoth or Aloth.

Anyway, the king gave full authority to Aloth to command and to order and to act and reckon without having to seek counsel for whatever he thought appropriate. And yet many of the nobles were dissatisfied with his governance because of the man's youth and his birth. As soon as the king heard these rumors and the reasons why most of the leading men were negligent in pursuing their enemies, he summoned a horse litter to take him to the field of battle. There he sent for those men who were indecisive about going into battle with Aloth, ordering them under pain of their vow of obedience to go with him to the battlefield, and this they willingly did. As they drew near the town of Brilianus, Octa and Offa and their men streamed out to confront Aloth, who gave them mighty battle on the field beside the town. A great number on both sides were killed, but in the end the Saxons had to turn and leave the field and flee to the town, around which Aloth and his men had placed careful sieges. But the disdain and jealousy and lack of obedience continued among the Britons. This gave great joy to the foreigners, who were informed daily about the jealousy and enmity within the ranks of the Britons. They also heard of the weakness of the king, who was coming to the battle in a *charrette* with additional men to maintain them in the siege. As soon as he came to the battlefield, he ordered machines to be put at the wall and men **(323r)** to dig ditches to undermine it and make everything ready for an assault. They all obeyed the order, as was appropriate. They set to work to weaken the wall, which was the power and strength of the Saxons.

The rumored disunity of the Britons and the weakness of their king gave the Saxons courage to sneak out of the town in the middle of the night with most of their people and strike heavily at the area where the king was. They knew well that he was so weak from his illness that he was capable of neither opposing his enemies with his own hand nor fleeing from their assault. The story says that there were three things that boosted their courage to try this plan. One was that they could see clearly that they would not be able to keep the town around them any longer, because of the lack and scarcity of many essentials such as food and equipment to defend the town. The second thing that was giving them courage to try this plan was that they could see clearly that if they were able to kill the king it would be easier to bring about their goal and their intention, especially because of the enmity and jealousy among the Britons. The third reason was that they could see clearly and without doubt that if their effort and their goal failed, it would be easier and more likely for them to be able to escape under cover of night than in the light of day. And on this plan and at the appointed time they crept out of the town, intending to catch the king and his men at rest, except for the night guards, at that time of night.

But despite the secrecy and quiet with which the Saxons prepared and executed this deceptive ambush, the king and his loyal council had received knowledge of their plan through their spies. And so the king ordered his men to remain in their harness as quietly as possible, which they did. When the right time of the night came, the Saxons crept silently out of the town, and when they got close to the place where the king was lying, they shouted out their cry to frighten the Britons, but these were at that moment in battle order and ready to fight. Immediately, the two hosts came together and a fierce battle ensued, in which, as my author (323v) writes, Octa and Offa were killed, along with a large number of Saxons. Those who escaped alive fled to Scottish lands, where after a time a large number of scoundrels from various peoples such as Saxons, Irish, and Scots gathered under a captain who was called Colgrim, the leader of these wicked people. They hoped privately that if they killed Uthyr and ended his life, they could get every sort of thing they wanted within his realm. And to attempt to destroy the king by guile and wicked means, they attempted various means and consulted a variety of men of cunning to seek to destroy him and so bring about their goals. But the Britons were not so careless that they would allow a foreigner to come near the king, for they did not forget that King Emrys had been poisoned not long before by the action of a foreigner.

They remained around the court, listening for what they could hear about the king, who was lying abed and nursing his illness in the town of Brilianus, which the Britons had won from the Saxons. In the meantime, spies had received word that the king was in his bed drinking only from a fountain whose water came from the grounds outside the town. Using his magic, a faithless traitor poisoned the well, and from that time the water poisoned the king and many of his nobles and commoners before anyone knew or suspected the water. But as soon as the king and his council heard how the accursed people had poisoned the well, they had a wall of stone built around it so that no man or animal could come close to it for many years afterward. From this poison Uthyr died, having been king for sixteen years. He was buried in the Cerrigle beside his brother Emrys.

MERLIN HELPS ARTHUR IN HIS EARLIEST BATTLES

NLW MS 5276Dii

The Chapel Perilous, site of Arthur's visions, appears in Malory's *Le morte d'Arthur* and in several modern works as a symbol of metaphysical occurrences.

(326v) After the death of Uthyr Pendragon, his son, Arthur, was crowned the king of the realm in the year of the age of Christ 517, which was the fifteenth year of his age and in the third year of the reign of Lotharios, the king of France. Shortly after his coronation and on Merlin's advice, Arthur went to the Perilous Chapel to consult the monk Masinus. At that time, the story says, Arthur saw angels saying mass. Immediately, Queen Mary appeared to him and asked him to destroy witchcraft and necromancy, which were very popular within the realm at that time. She gave him a cross of gold, which she asked him to keep around him when he went onto the field of battle. And so, according to some of the writings, Arthur carried a blue shield and a cross of gold, with an image of Mary in the upper corner of the shield. And after this he took a vow to destroy his enemies and the necromancers and the sorcerers. And soon after that, he raised a large host of Britons, whom he led to the north against Colgrim, who had brought a large host of Saxons to Lindsey and then conquered the land and the town of Caer Llwydcoed. The king led all the men he could to that place. In the meantime, Colgrim and his people took control of a large field and fortified it strongly with ditches and dikes to resist and give battle to Arthur. When the two forces confronted each other and the day of the encounter had been determined, some of the accounts say that Merlin caused Arthur to give an order to all the chieftains of his forces to make banners of white silk and lace and a red cross in the middle of them. This they all **(327r)** did. And when this had been done, Arthur and his men struck against the enemy, and a fierce and cruel battle ensued. Arthur succeeded in killing a great number of the pagans in the battle, and in the end he won the fortress from which

Colgrim had fled, he and as many of his men who had escaped alive, to the north. There they took the strong walls of Caer Efrog to defend themselves from the savagery of Arthur and the Britons, who mounted a merciless siege around the fort. Colgrim furtively escaped from there and crossed the sea to Childeric [II], the king of the Germans.

ARTHUR AND THE SWORD IN THE STONE

NLW MS 5276Dii

This story is well known to readers at all levels and to moviegoers as well. The few additional details in this account humanize it beyond its magical overtones.

(325r) After the death of Uthyr Pendragon son of Custennin there arose conflict among the princes of the realm over the succession to the kingship. Many of the authors say that few of the princes accepted Arthur as the son of Uthyr, and others say that none of them even knew that he had a son. And because of this situation, as Geoffrey and other authors say, God eventually worked miracles to validate for the people that Arthur was worthy to wear the crown and rule the realm. This is what God did. He sent a marble stone to the church at Caerwynt, in which there was (325v) embedded a sword standing alongside the cross. And these words were inscribed on the hilt of the sword: "Whoever can pull this out of the stone is worthy to be king." All the chieftains of the realm were summoned to attempt to pull the sword from the stone. But some of the books say that it was to Caer Ludd that God sent the stone and the sword, but it doesn't matter to which city the sword was sent, because all the writers agree that all the chieftains of the realm came to where the stone was. Some of the writers say that the stone was plucked from the ground and put on a scaffold where everyone and those who were trying to pull the sword from it could see it. Others say that the stone, the sword, and the scaffold stood within the church. But it matters not, since all the authors agree that all the chieftains tried to pull the sword from the stone, and every one of them failed to do so.

At the time of this huge gathering, as my author shows, a dispute and hostility arose between the son of Cynnydd Gain Farfog, Arthur's foster father, and a nobleman in the crowd. And this argument resulted in a hand-to-hand fight between the two. But other writers have claimed that it was but playful sport and jousting between a nobleman and a foster brother of Arthur's when his sword fell away. But I have not seen any evidence at all as to whether it was a fight or play that was going on when the sword fell away, for all the authors' accounts agree that Arthur's foster brother asked Arthur to fetch a sword, whether for sport or for combat. Arthur went straight to the stone and pulled the sword quickly and easily and took it to his foster brother. As soon as the foster brother saw the writing on the hilt, he cried at the top of his voice, "'Tis I who am worthy of the crown, I who will be king!" These words stunned all the nobles and commoners **(326r)** who heard them. But after all the wise men saw him with the sword in his hand, they had him brought before the stone and instructed him to put the sword back so that the nobles and the entire crowd could see him pulling it out of the stone. The lad returned the sword easily to the stone with one hand, but using both hands and with all his strength he could not draw it out again. Finally, he told them how he had gotten the sword from Arthur, his foster brother. So they summoned Arthur before them in front of the stone where the sword stood. Here, as my source says, the nobles had Arthur pull the sword from the stone and put it back again three or four times in the presence of all the assembled nobles so that they might all see him pull the sword from the stone. And so every one of them could see clearly that God had chosen and selected Arthur to be the king.

THE DEATH OF MERLIN

NLW MS 5276Dii

Death is not quite the right word for the fate of Merlin recorded here. The Glassy Isle and the perilous bridge are the stuff of medieval romance and are places where life is eternal. But more than that, Merlin is said to live at least up to the time of Maelgwn Gwynedd. And as we see from other stories in this collection, Taliesin and Merlin are confused in the tradition so that, as is recounted here, Merlin was known as Taliesin in the time of Maelgwn.

(351r) A short while after this, Merlin left the court of the king and met his beloved near Glyn Galabes, where he had fallen in love with a noblewoman of that district. She, as the story of the San Greal says, was a clever and learned woman, and she saw clearly that he was of a devilish (351v) nature, so in no way did she bend to his will but did promise him from day to day that under certain conditions she would be ready to do his bidding. The conditions were that he teach her all his arts and learning perfectly by such and such a day and time. And on those conditions they agreed. And from then on, he spent his time making a house of glass for them to live in forever and teaching his arts to his beloved. All this he did quickly. And after the bower or house was ready, he told her that he had fully completed her conditions, both teaching her and building the bower. Some of the books say that he built it in a place called Ynys Wydrin, "Glassy isle," which opened onto a perilous bridge and is in Sir Caerloyw, Gloucestershire. Eventually, he brought his beloved to the bower, opened the door, and urged her to go inside. But the story says that she had knowledge that the door was so ingeniously constructed that no one could open it once it had been closed. Because of that, she was loath to go inside, even though she had heard that the bower was so heavenly wrought inside that they would never lack for food or drink but live there like angels forever. Indeed, this story is unlike the truth, for it stands with neither reason nor faith. But anyway, we will follow the story, which says that there was great deference between (352r) Merlin and his beloved as to who would go in first. He wanted her to enter before him, and she wanted him to go in first. After some discussion, she prevailed. As soon as she got him through the door, she pulled the door to her and closed it tightly. Thereupon the bower disappeared, with Merlin inside, and no one knew where on earth or in the firmament it went.

And this is how Merlin disappeared. Yet some of the writers say that it was in the rocks of Brittany that his beloved hid Merlin when he had become old and that after this she was a lady of great powers in the land of Gascony, where, as the story of the San Greal says, she magically surrounded her entire realm with a body of water. Because of that she was called in French and in English "the Lady of the Lake." But even so, Geoffrey of Monmouth says that from fear for her life she fled from the island to Gascony, from fear of the people who kept calling about Merlin. But it doesn't matter why she went from this island, because all the stories agree that she was the Lady of the Lake and that she raised Lancelot of the Lake in that place. But it seems strange to me to allow that a man as wise and clever and a prophet as good as so many people believe that Merlin was would let a woman best him in his own art. And yet there are (352v) many opinions and much talk among people, for many of them hold the opinion and aver firmly that Merlin was a spirit in human form that had been in this shape from the time of Gwrtheyrn to the days of King Arthur, when he vanished. But then this spirit returned in the time of Maelgwn Gwynedd, at which time he was called Taliesin. It is said that he was living again in a city called Caer Sidia, whence he appeared a third time, in the days of Morfryn Frych, whose son he was said to be, and in this age he was called Merlin Wyllt, "Wild." But in spite of all this, to this day he is said to be reposed in Caer Sidia, whence some people firmly believe he will rise up once more before Judgment Day. And indeed, I believe this story to be true, for it is widely known throughout Wales and in England too. It shows at length that astronomical learning was alive in the city of Caer Ludd in the old days, and some of the books say that it was Merlin, and others say that it was another astronomer. But it doesn't matter which one it was, because the books agree completely that this astronomer said secretly to one of his neighbors that whoever takes his beans and sows them on a certain day and hour on this island in a field of the sort that is now called a "long" field, that which lies on the north side of the road that leads from Charing Cross to Strond, there will (353r) grow from them profitable beans, assuring the man that their stalks would be silver and their pods gold. And from his lust for gold, the man to whom the astronomer told the story rented this land and sowed his beans on the day and time that the astronomer had indicated. Sometime later, he instructed the man to cut them when they were full of the fruit of gold and silver.

And after the astronomer and the laborer harvested them into sheaves of gold and silver, the astronomer had the man dig a deep hole in a secret place beside the piece of land, saying that there would never be the ability or power to uncover any of this hiding place until a time when there would be the big field in Charing Cross. At that time, this wealth would be used to enrich the poor of the realm forever from that time on. And to confirm that this story is as true as though the sea were seething, it is told among the old people around Caer Ludd about certain men who went to dig a foundation for the bell tower of the church that lies between Charing Cross and the aforementioned piece of land. This was in the time of Henry VII. At the time, the workers heard a voice or a vehement sound that said fiercely that they must not dig any closer in that place. And the word was that they must not dig in that place any deeper. *Finit.*

HUAIL SON OF CAW AND ARTHUR

NLW MS 5276Dii

Caw of Prydyn was a late-fifth-to-early-sixth-century ruler of north Britain. Among his many progeny were the scholar-saint Gildas, the author of *De excidio et conquestu Britanniae*, and the considerably less eminent Huail. This story is no less interesting as the only narrative in which Arthur cross-dresses. Typically, perhaps, it ends on an onomastic note.

(329v–330r) Some of the stories say that in the land today called Edeirnion there lived a nobleman named Caw or, as some of the books call him, Caw of Britain. He had two sons, the older of whom was called Gildas son of Caw. He was a famous scholar who preached and wrote many books that are praised among scholars up to the present day. The second son was named Huail son of Caw, who was lustful and wanton. The story says that he turned his vulgarity and affection on one of Arthur's concubines. Arthur became jealous and went secretly to the concubine's house and waited outside to kill Huail. Huail came there, and Arthur was waiting; after much talk, they came together with their swords and fought like lions. After much fighting, Huail managed to land a blow on one of Arthur's knees, wounding him badly. But anyway, the story says that Arthur and Huail came to an agreement before they left that place, the condition being that Huail would not reproach Arthur for that blow under pain of losing his head. And so they departed, and Arthur went home to his court, which was in a town that the San Greal says was called Caer Haas, which according to the story is now called Caerwys, where he was healed of his wound, from which, as the story says, he was a bit lame all his life.

A while after his wound healed, Arthur became enamored of a girl from the town of Rhuthun. He went there after disguising himself in a woman's clothing. Huail happened to see him dancing among the girls and recognized him from his limp. As he watched Arthur, he said, "The dancing is quite good were it not for the bad knee." Arthur heard that, and he knew that those words were said to mock him. So Arthur left the company and secretly went to his court. He had Huail brought before him and accused him of breaking his vow. After many words, Arthur ordered him seized and taken to the marketplace, where his head was cut off on a stone that lay in the middle of the road. This was all accomplished in due course. And to help remember the event, that stone has ever since been called Huail's Stone.

ARTHUR DREAMS OF THE LOSS OF KINGSHIP

NLW MS 5276Dii

As we have seen from the history of Merlin and his sister, Gwenddydd, dreams require the accurate recall of the dreamer and the magic of the interpreter to be deciphered. Time may often be of the essence, but in this case extreme steps have to be taken to extract meaning from such nighttime apparitions.

(330r) At this time, according to some of the stories, Arthur made his court in a place now called Nannerch, and the place is still called Arthur's Court. And it is said that his chapel in the church was long afterward called Capel Gwial ["Chapel of the scepter"]. And in that quarter of the realm, Arthur and his soldiers fought many battles, especially in the place that the story of the San Greal calls Ystrett Mares, a place that the story supposes is the place today called Ystrad March as far as Eurloes, or Ynys Fon. Also the story says that at the time, King Arthur had a remarkable dream. He imagined in his sleep that he saw all the hair on his head fall to the ground and all his fingers and toes except the thumbs and big toes fall off. This stunned the king greatly. He had a large number of the most learned men and those of the greatest judgment in such visions summoned and charged them with showing him within a few days what the dream meant. He put them into a secure prison, where they were kept for a time without finding out (330v) anything. They couldn't understand at all what the dream signified. So Arthur ordered that they all be punished. But eventually they told him that they had seen that he had lost his kingship. He asked them what remedy and help they saw that would help prevent that fate and that vision. They answered at length and told him that they had seen that there was help to withstand the misfortune that faced him but that they were unable to show him what it was because the things that would help were so bizarre. They were a lion in water, the intercession of a flower, and the advice of an old person.

And so Arthur went off to hunt in the area now called Denbighshire. There he pursued a wild animal so intently that he became separated from his people and lost his way. It happened that he saw the footprints of a large animal and those of a person following it. He kept on until he came to a cave in a rock where he saw the tracks of the person and the animal leading into the cave. He followed them in. Inside he found three exceedingly large and very ugly people, a hag and her son and daughter conversing politely among themselves. The hag and her son wanted to kill Arthur, but the maiden would not allow it, patiently allowing him to leave blameless if he could remember three true sayings and repeat them in their presence on the following morning. The story says that they allowed Arthur to remain free, and when the time came for them to go to bed, the son made Arthur lie on the ground and laid an animal skin over him, which, the story says, was so heavy that Arthur was not strong enough to rise up under it. And when morning (331r) came, the son lifted the skin from Arthur and asked him to stand. Then the son took up his harp and played beautifully. The hag asked him when he would like to recite the three true sayings. "Whenever you want me to say them," he replied. And thereupon the son ceased playing the harp and asked him to recite.

"The first of the three sayings," he said, "is that you are the best harper I have ever heard." "That's true," said the hag. "And the second true saying is that you are the ugliest and most monstrous two people that I have ever seen, you and your mother." "That's true," said the hag. "And the third true saying is if I were outside this rocky hole I would never enter it again as long as I lived." "And having fulfilled that condition," said the hag, "you are free to leave, blameless."

And that is how the king lost his kingship, because another man cannot rightfully name or call himself the king while a king is in prison and captivity—whence he, the rightful king, was set free through the strength of the lion and his power, which clever storytellers substitute for the power and might of God, who walks through the entire world, through water and land alike. And the maiden was the flower, who entreated her brother to let him live.

But the story of the San Greal explains the dream differently, saying that it was in the field that was between him and King Gawnes and

King Surloes that the dream occurred. At the time, as the story says, King Arthur was being very careful about choosing the people to stand against his enemies, for there were many of his people who were negligent in following him into the field because of some animosity between them and the king, due to his bad leadership. At this time, a monk came to the king and chastised him sternly for his bad leadership. It was to him **(331v)** that the king revealed his dream and all that had passed between him and the diviners and their answers to him about a remedy for his misfortune. At that, the monk berated the king at length, as much for trusting in diviners whose learning and practice were against the knowledge and law that had made him king. And because of the wrongful conduct of his life, the Heavenly Father threatened to take away his kingship. And then the monk explained the king's dream in this way: "The hair you saw falling from your head signifies the common people of the realm, who are withdrawing their love and affection from you because of your meanness and your miserliness. And the toes of your feet and fingers of your hands represent your nobles of every grade, whose love for you has ceased, all except three or four who are following the same deceitful ways as you, and these are signified by the thumbs of your hands and big toes of your feet. And indeed, were it not for the lion in water that the diviners said was helping you, you would lose your kingship. Human opinions and worldly reason did not allow them to understand this, which is that the lion was the power of God and the flower was Mary."

ARTHUR AND THE ROUND TABLE

NLW MS 5276Dii

The Round Table has been one of the preeminent symbols of the kingship of Arthur from the Middle Ages to the modern era. The idea, of course, was to ensure equality among the chief knights of his court. The table's origins, however, are not entirely clear. Elis's version—or the one he accepts—follows here. Especially interesting is that Arthur's enemy King Gawnes was made one of the knights of the Round Table.

(331v) Shortly after this, Arthur and his men went to battle against King Gawnes. In the field with Gawnes was Lancelot du Lac, who was fighting on his side against Arthur. But the story of the San Greal says that King Gawnes had made Lancelot swear an oath to do whatever he asked of him, to come to the battlefield and fight under his banner on this day. Lancelot obeyed, and through his fighting prowess and bravery the kings Gawnes and Surloes overcame most of the forces of Arthur, who had mostly lost the battle. An earlier story says that the queen [Gwenhwyfar], who was (332r) on the other side of the river watching the battlefield, was urging certain men who were around the king to encourage him to flee with them when they saw the battle was being lost. Those men were waiting every minute for the chance to turn their backs and flee with their leaders from the field, for they could see that Arthur and his men had lost the battle.

At that moment, Lancelot turned to King Gawnes and said to him, "You see, Noble King, that I have made good my oath and your wishes. And now I ask you to make good your promise and my own wish—to wit, I ask Your Grace to ride with me unarmed through the host until you come with me to where Arthur is, then dismount your horse, kneel down, and submit to Arthur, asking his mercy and forgiveness for the tumult and vexation you have continued to cause him right up to today." This both King Gawnes and King Surloes did willingly. And this is how Lancelot kept Arthur's kingship, his respect, and his honor, through the miracles of God. And the San Greal says that King Gawnes was the king over twenty-two realms, whose kings were conquered and subjugated by him and served him on the battlefield, all of whom then swore fealty to Arthur. In exchange for this, Arthur made King Gawnes one of the knights of the Round Table, the highest order there was at that time. And the story mentioned earlier shows that Arthur instituted law and order so that it was not legal or praiseworthy for any of his men to engage in combat unless it was one against one, and this included all the nobles of the realm, those who were against him as well as those who were his own men. He also decreed that all his knights and soldiers must make an oath in the presence of the entire court when one of them was going in quest of adventure, to return to Arthur's court by the end of a day and a year if he was living and (332v) his feet were free and to give a true report to the king's scholars of every sort of adventure that had been experienced on the quest, so that one of the four scholars could write them down. These, as the story of the San Greal says, were Cowdrws of Verselys, Tomas of Tuletto, Herodian of Gulen, and the fourth was Sappiers

Bawdas, the four who wrote down all the adventures of Arthur and his soldiers.

After this, Arthur and his soldiers overcame all the oppressors of the realm, as well as men who had not yet been made free. Later, Arthur took his men in ships and sailed from this island to Ireland, where, as the story shows at some length, he overcame Gwilmor, the king of the island, and he and his lords submitted to Arthur and pledged fealty to him. They were true and obedient to Arthur from that time on. The story then says that he and his men took to the ships again and set sail from there to the land of Yaf, whose king and people he conquered. After that, he established every element of rule and stability for true guardianship of the island under his lordship. Then he took his men and sailed from there to the land called Suthland, which he conquered and set up under conservatorship in that same way. Geoffrey says that King Arthur tarried in the land and the area and in his conquest for as long as twelve years, during which time word of his and his soldiers' deeds and of his largesse and his nobility spread across the face of the earth equally to the great majority of the nobles of Europe as well as to the principal ones and the very best of them in his court and in his service. And according to the opinion of some of the authors, there were so many knights in the court of King (333r) Arthur at that time that no one could judge who was bravest, who was noblest, whose feats were best, so that, as the story says, quarrels grew in Arthur's court over the seating arrangements at mealtimes. To resolve this, Arthur had a round table made, so that every sort of knight who could compete in nobility and deeds could sit so that each one was as high as the others. And this is how at that time the Round Table and its order were begun. But some authors say that King Uthyr Pendragon was the first to make a round table for knights of privilege and nobility to sit at.

THE FINAL BATTLE, ARTHUR DIES

NLW MS 5276Dii

(336r) After Arthur established governance for everything in the realm, he made his nephew Mordred the earl of Cornwall and keeper and defender of the realm. . . .

(338v) . . . But as the story says, ever since Arthur and his hosts left the kingdom, Mordred had been the keeper and defender of this island. Night and day during this time he was thinking how he could be king. All the authors say that he was an evil, wanton, covetous person bent on achieving what he lusted for, the thing he constantly wished for more than anything else: the head of King Arthur seven cubits under the ground. Eventually, this became known among the king's closest friends, who quickly sent word to Arthur about Mordred's determination to be the king and about the treachery of Gwenhwyfar: some of the authors say she encouraged and emboldened Mordred to pretend to the kingship. Soon Mordred realized his ambition, by giving a huge sum of money to Cerdicus, the king of the Saxons of the West, to support him in gaining the crown of the realm.

Some of the books say that Mordred was crowned the king of all of Britain in Caer Ludd and that Cerdicus was crowned the king of the Saxons of the West in Caerwynt. At that time, Mordred gave him Sussex and Suthre, where Ella and his three sons had been kings. And the authors say that Mordred and Cerdicus and Gwenhwyfar sent certain emissaries to Denmark and to the Saxons requesting that the nobles of the realms and kingdoms send them so many warriors to defend them against King Arthur and those who stood with him.

When King Arthur heard the truth of these plans, he felt anger and great rage toward them all, for their treacherous behavior in conspiring to deprive him of his sovereignty over the **(339r)** Isle of Britain and for their wickedness in causing him to abort his plans of going to take possession of Rome, where he and his soldiers were hastily headed. Arthur turned his troops around quickly, and with great effort he led them in the most direct and quickest way back to this island. He had them embark from Flanders, according to some of the authors, but other writers say that it was from a town now called Whitson, which lies between Calais and Bwlen, which was a harbor capable of handling a thousand great ships. It was at that time that his troops embarked, and it doesn't matter where he boarded his ships, because all the authors agree that it was in the place now called the Downs, which lies beside the town of Sandwich, where he and his people landed.

Mordred and his army came there intending to prevent Arthur from coming ashore. There, as some of the British authors say, Mordred had his leading archers shoot arrows without tips on them, so that Arthur might understand clearly that it was not of his will or intent to rise up against him or to do the things that he had done. But it doesn't matter which it was of the two, whether of his own will and desire or not, that he had turned against Arthur, because the story says that they fought a hard battle as they came to shore. Gawen was killed and many nobles, along with many French people who had come in support of King Arthur. By dint of great effort, Arthur gained the land, with no thanks to Mordred and his men. They fled when they lost the battle, passing through the land of Caer Gangen, intent on reaching the stronghold of Caer Ludd until more men could join him, from both Denmark and the Saxons and those who were coming with them. But the citizens **(339v)** of Caer Ludd closed the stronghold's gates against him, so Mordred fled once again, with Cerdicus, the king of the Saxons of the West, to Caerwynt, where they were allowed to come from the aforementioned places.

During this time, King Arthur was busy and at pains to unload the brigantine to ready the troops to pursue the enemy and to see to the burial of those who had been killed in the battle. He had the body of Gawen and the bodies of the nobles brought to Dover Castle, where, as some of the books say, there was a monastery of Black Friars. And he had the body of Anglicius, the king of the Scots, sent to his own land, where he was buried with honor. When he had put everything in order, he hastened to Caerwynt.

Meanwhile, Gwenhwyfar was holding court in York Castle when word came to her that Arthur and his men had landed, no thanks to Mordred, who needed his men at Caerwynt, and also that the cities and towns were turning against Mordred. This news caused her much sadness, for she could see that if Arthur won she would not get much mercy. And so she gathered as many men in harness as she could find in that part of the country, along with all of the foreigners who had come there from Denmark and Saxony, and embarked with them along the sea to Cornwall. Some of the books say that she went with the rest in ships to Cornwall and then went secretly with two or three others from there to a house of religious women to Caerllion ar Wysg. But others claim that she went in secret by land from Caer Efrog to Caerllion. But it matters not which of the two ways she traveled to Caerllion, because they say that she was in a **(340r)** nunnery from that time for as long as she lived.

Arthur and his men laid siege to Caerwynt, where Mordred and Cerdicus and their hosts had retreated and battled with Arthur yet again. Arthur got the best of them, and Mordred and Cerdicus fled from there to Cornwall, where the foreigners had landed from places where they had gathered a great host in countless numbers. They came against King Arthur, who had also assembled a great many men. The two hosts finally met in a narrow field beside the monastery of Glastonbury. Then, after the two armies had been drawn up ready to join in combat, Mordred sent a herald to the king, asking him to parley with him before the hosts began to fight. The king quickly agreed. A place for them to stand and talk was chosen, atop a mound between the two armies so that all could see them clearly. The two were warned not to make any move toward the other lest they be seen to be fighting. And so the two armies stood facing each other, with the two leaders between them atop the mound. They conversed for some time, but the writer does not say what they discussed. But he does say that a most remarkable thing occurred as they were about to part from each other. The story says that as were leaving, apparently under an agreement that they were willing to quit the battlefield until a time when they could discuss the matter further, Mordred saw an ugly-looking insect sitting on the cap under Arthur's helmet. He seized his sword quickly, intent on killing the insect, and poked at the king's cap. The insect sprung from there onto Mordred's head, whereupon Arthur drew his sword, intending to kill the **(340v)** insect where it landed on Mordred's head. And so each of them dealt a blow to the other, unmindful of the promise they had made to the two armies. The hosts clashed, fighting the moment when they saw their two leaders striking each other. Soon Mordred and Arthur were fighting like two fierce lions, and the story says that each of them killed the other. Arthur struck Mordred dead on the battlefield, and Mordred wounded Arthur in the thigh, from which Arthur died a short while later, as this work shows. And the authors say that the fighting of the two parties was so fierce and so brutal that none of the famous combatants in the battle survived, except one of the chieftains, who grieved pitifully, for if the stories of the battle can be believed, the flower and glory of all the great ones of every realm and kingship were killed in that battle. . . .

(342r) Some of the authors say and firmly believe that Arthur will rise again to be the king. They are of the opinion and say that he is sleeping in a cave under a mountain near Glastonbury. And indeed, if it can be believed, various people from that area have said that he has appeared and then vanished to many people and in many wonderful ways for three hundred years.

ARTHUR'S CAVE FOUND

NLW MS 3054Dii

As the opening lines show, this text does not follow the preceding stories chronologically, nor is it in the same part of the manuscript, but it is appropriately placed here.

(451r) In the year of the age of Christ 1518 until 1524 there were many wondrous stories among the kingdom's common people. Some spoke of seeing a variety of weird visions, such as men fighting in two armies on some fields in western parts. Also in the vicinity of Gloucester, people spoke of seeing some of Arthur's soldiers. They followed them to the mouth of a cave where they could see an old man sleeping in a splendid bed. This, they were told, was King Arthur. The story was so strange and so widespread that it came to the ears of the king, who sent some servants to listen to the story. It was about a woman riding on the back of a magnificent horse—it wasn't clear if she was coming from a mill or a market. If the story is true, she encountered one of Arthur's servants, who asked her if she would sell her horse. After some discussion, she agreed, and the specter led her to a court the likes of which she had never seen. She said she saw there an immeasurable number of people sleeping and of horses in a stable. Her horse was put in with the others after the man had paid her for it and given her a horse to carry her home. After the man had taken her outside the cave, he vanished and left her standing there like a person waking from her sleep after seeing a dream and not knowing at all where she had been. She went home to her husband. The kind of stamp on the money was such that that no one in that land could read the inscription. And this I believe to be true, because there was not on them any kind of known stamp more fraudulent, and in my view and judgment this story is as false as rocks talking or the sea burning. But anyway, there are many sensible men in the king's court and in the realm who believe that these stories are as true as the Lord's Prayer.

CHARLEMAGNE AND ARTHUR

NLW MS 5276Dii

Charlemagne was the king of the Franks from 768 to 814 and the first ruler of the Holy Roman Empire, starting in 800. This story is set in Aachen (then Aquae Granni), where Charlemagne spent much time. Turpin, an eighth-century bishop of Rheims, was the author of a history of Charlemagne. Saint Augustine of Hippo wrote his *Civitas Dei* (*City of God*) in the fifth century.

(455r) Charlemagne built a temple to Mary in the city of Aachen toward the end of his life. At that time, as Turpin says in his history, the emperor devoted his time to reading religious works, such as the book called *City of God* and various other books by Saint Augustine. But other authors say that he devoted himself to books of fighting and battles and the deeds of doughty knights. At the time, he sent to this island for books of Arthur and his knights. Dr. Alfimus delivered to him all the stories of Arthur and his knights completely. As a result, there are more stories of Arthur and his soldiers among the French than among the Britons and the Saxons.

III

Tales of Magic, Prophecy, and the Supernatural

MAELGWN GWYNEDD, HIS WIFE, AND THE RING

NLW MS 5276Dii

Maelgwn was the king of Gwynedd in the early half of the sixth century; he died in 547 (*pace* the date below). A powerful ruler, he held court mostly at Degannwy in Conwy county in north Wales. This narrative brings us into the milieu of that other master of the arts Taliesin, a contemporary, as it were, of Merlin.

(361v) Maelgwn Gwynedd was made the king after Vortiporius. Some of the books say that he was the son of Vortiporius, and others say that Maelgwn was the son of Caswalldan Lawhir, one of the nobles of Gwynedd. And yet despite this, some of the Welsh books say that he was not kin to either of these three [*sic*] or to any of the three who had ruled Gwynedd in succession some time before this. They were, as I have seen in some old Welsh books, Rhydderch Hael, Morgan son **(362r)** of Sadwrn, and Urien son of Cynfarch. But anyway, it matters not whose son he was and only shows the differences and disagreements that go into the work of those writing history, since each of them agrees that Maelgwn was crowned the king of the Britons in the year of Christ 552. These, as the author of a florilegium says, were within the nearly twenty-two years of the reign of Lotharius, the king of the Franks. And they show that Maelgwn was capable and victorious and gained the upper hand over the Saxons in numerous battles and won much land from his enemies in the north and west of this island. And with the wealth from the spoils of his enemies, he had four strong castles built to protect his people. The first of these he had built on the shore of the Hafren, to keep the Saxons in England. He called it Caer Digoll, now called Amwythig. The second town he built on the Irish Sea at the place where foreigners often come to shore. This he named Caer Collwyn, today known as Harddlech. The third he had built on the shore of the river now known as Conwy, which he named Caer Cyffin and today is called Aberconwy. The fourth castle that Maelgwn Gwynedd built was on the other side of the river, near the sea, to protect the narrow part of the river from foreigners coming to land there. He called the place Caer Deganwy and built a strong castle there; he used to hold court in it often, (362v) and some of the walls are still standing. Some of the books hold that he married the daughter of Saul Benuchel, and the story says that from her he had a son called Enion or Einion and a daughter named Eurgain. The Welsh books say that she married a powerful baron from the north as old as her father, and some of them say that she bore him a son who was called Elidir and another, illegitimate, son called Rhun.

The stories about Maelgwn tell that his queen went out one day to take her pleasure wandering among the rocks and cliffs that lie along the Conwy River. As she did so, it happened that her ring, the dearest and most treasured that she and the king possessed, slipped from her finger and rolled over the rocks and into the sea, where there was no chance of retrieving it. This caused her much grief and concern. Worried that the king might ask her about the ring, she sent word to Asaph son of Saul Benuchel, her brother, who was the bishop in Llanelwy then, asking him to come and break the news to the king and tell him of the unfortunate accident, how she happened to lose the ring. She feared that the king would suppose the worst, for the story says that he was one of the most jealous persons in the world.

(363r) As soon as the bishop received his sister's request, he arranged a feast to which he invited the king and queen. Immediately after the king arrived at the bishop's court in Llanelwy, the bishop explained to the king the manner in which the queen had lost her ring. The king became enraged and said many angry and jealous things to the bishop and his sister the queen. That troubled the bishop greatly, causing him to pray for God's grace to help him convince the king about how she had lost the ring.

The story says that as the bishop and his sister sat there depressed, it happened that a local fisherman caught a large salmon, which he carried straight to the court and gave as a present to the king. The king had it taken to the cook and ordered that it be prepared for dinner. The cook did so, and as he cut open the fish he found a ring in its belly. Surprised at this, the cook put the fish belly with the ring inside on a plate and placed it before the king. As soon as he saw the ring and recognized it, he asked the queen's forgiveness for blaming her. Then he sent for the bishop, to whom he gave land and territory. And because he saw how the Heavenly Father, through his prayers, brought the ring back, he gave the land to the holy bishop, who, with Maelgwn's help, built the bishop's palace of Llanelwy, and the church today is called the Church (363v) of Asaph, and his body is buried in the place where the aforementioned ring is kept. And the authors Guido and Geoffrey agree that Maelgwn was one of the purest, gentlest, and bravest there ever was in this realm.

THE STORY OF GWION BACH

NLW MS 5276Dii

This story accounts for the origin of Taliesin, who is later confused with Merlin. The account of his remarkable birth and subsequent arcane powers begins, as noted below, at folio 353 in Elis's chronicle. The next folio is no longer extant; the lost material is supplied here from the 1609 manuscript of John Jones of Gellilyfdy, who had copied this part of Elis's chronicle before the folio went missing and the others were numbered. For the details of the transmission of the Gwion Bach story, see my *Ystoria Taliesin* (Cardiff: University of Wales Press, 1992). The story accounts for the remarkable powers of prophecy and magic in the later career of Taliesin, imparted by herbs and plants through the person of Gwion Bach and the womb of the witch Ceridwen.

(353r) There follows here the story of Gwion Bach, which is widely known in Wales. In the early days of Arthur, there was a nobleman called Tegid Foel living in the area now known as Penllyn. (353v) His own patrimony, as the story tells, was a body of water now called Llyn Tegid, "Tegid's lake." The story says he had a wife called Ceridwen, and it says that she was learned and skilled in the arts—namely, magic, witchcraft, and sorcery. It relates further that Ceridwen and Tegid had a male child and that he was most disagreeable in appearance and behavior. And so he was named Morfran, "Great crow," and later, because of his color, Y Fagddu, "The dark lad." His mother lamented the boy's gloomy appearance, knowing that there was no way or means for her son to be accepted among the noblemen unless he had qualities other than his appearance. To accomplish this, she turned her mind entirely to contemplating her arts to discover the best way that she could make him full of the spirit of prophecy and knowledge about the world to come.

After laboring long in her arts, she saw that the way to achieve such knowledge lay in the plants and herbs of the earth and one's labor and cunning—to wit, gather a large amount of certain herbs and plants of the earth on special days and times, put them all in a caldron of water, put the caldron on the fire, and keep it boiling continually night and day for a year and a day. At the end of that time she would see clearly that three drops **(end of 353v)** containing all the qualities of the many herbs and plants would spring forth. On whatever man these three drops fell, she knew that that one would be skilled in the various arts and full of the spirit of prophecy. She also knew that all of the juice from these plants except for those three drops would be the most powerful poison in the world. It would shatter the caldron and send the poison across the land.

Indeed, this account is contrary to reason and against faith and sanctity. But still, the bulk of the story says that she gathered a great many plants of the earth, put them into a caldron of water, and set it on the fire. The story says that she had an old blind man to stir and turn it, but it doesn't give the name of the man any more than the name of the author of this story. But the story does name the lad who was leading the old man, and that is Gwion Bach, and Ceridwen set him to keeping the fire going under the caldron. And so each of them kept at their tasks, tending to the fire, stirring and refining the caldron, and Ceridwen keeping it full of water and plants to the end of a day and a year.

At that time, Ceridwen took her son, Morfran, and placed him close to the caldron so he could receive the drops when the time came for them to spring from the caldron. Then Ceridwen reclined to rest her legs and fell asleep at the moment when the three magical drops sprang from the caldron. They fell upon Gwion Bach, who had pushed Morfran out of the way. Thereupon the caldron gave a scream and broke apart from the potency of the poison. The scream woke Ceridwen from her sleep, and like a crazed person she espied Gwion Bach, who was now full of wisdom and could see clearly that she was of such a poisonous nature that she would punish him as soon as she found out that he had deprived her son of the magical drops. And so he took to his feet and fled.

As soon as Ceridwen came to her right mind, she asked her son what had happened. He told her in some detail how Gwion drove him from where she had placed him to stand. And so she raced from the house like a crazed woman in pursuit of Gwion, whom she saw fleeing in the shape of a hare. She turned herself into a black greyhound and followed him from place to place. Finally, after long pursuit in various shapes, she was so strong on him that he had to flee into a barn, where there was a huge mound of winnowed wheat. There he turned himself into one of the grains. But Ceridwen changed herself into a small black hen, and in that shape she swallowed Gwion into her belly, where she carried him for nine months, at which time she gave birth to him.

When she looked at him after bringing him into the world, she could neither do him bodily harm with her own hand nor let (354r) anyone else harm him in her presence. At last she had him put into a coracle, or hide-bound basket, which she made watertight both above and below. She put the child into it and cast him into the lake, as some of the books say. But other say that he was put into a river, and still others say that he was put into the sea, where he was found long after, as this work will show in due course.

THE EPIPHANY OF TALIESIN

NLW MS 5276Dii

Details of the function of court poets in Wales, as articulated in this story, can also be found in a number of historical Welsh documents. Maelgwn's chief poet is called Henin Fardd, "Henin poet." The name may contain the adjective *hen*, "old," plus an adjective suffix, so it may mean simply "ancient or original, ancestral poet." That is certainly fitting for the most important figure in Maelgwn's court. As it turns out in the story, however, Taliesin is far superior to Henin and in fact can therefore be seen as the "chief" poet of the court. As we read further on, Taliesin is called Merlin by John the Divine, and it's not difficult to see

Merlin/Taliesin as the prime poet of Maelgwn's court. The birth tales of both Merlin and Taliesin recount unusual pregnancies and unusual dispositions of the newborns and their fosterage. The several arcane songs that Taliesin sings are omitted here, but the texts may be found in my edition of *Ystoria Taliesin* (Cardiff: University of of Wales Press, 1992) and their translations in my *The Mabinogi and Other Medieval Welsh Tales* (Berkeley: University of California Press, 1977).

(364r) When Maelgwn Gwynedd was holding court at Deganwy there was a holy man named Cybi living in Môn [Ynys Fon]. And there was a wealthy squire named Gwyddno Garanhir living near Deganwy. He kept a weir between the shore of the Conwy River and the sea, and every Calan Gaeaf, November 1, ten pounds' worth of salmon was caught in that weir. Gwyddno had a son, Elphin, who was a courtier in Maelgwn's court. The story says that he was noble and generous and much in favor among his friends. But he was also lavish and wasteful, like most of the **(364v)** courtiers. As long as Gwyddno's money lasted, Elphin could continue his lavish way with his friends. But as his wealth declined, Gwyddno stopped supplying his son with money. Elphin complained to his friends that he was no longer able to support them as he had done formerly, for his father had fallen into poverty. So he asked some of the courtiers to ask for the catch of fish for him on the next Calan Gaeaf. This they did, and Gwyddno granted their request.

And so when that day came, Elphin took some servants with him to see to the weir, which was maintained from flood tide to ebb. When Elphin and his men went into the weir, they found neither head nor tail of salmon, where normally it would be full on that night. But the story says that all he saw there was some dark object caught within the arms of the weir. He bowed his head and began to curse his misfortune, saying as he turned homeward that he was the unluckiest man in the whole world. Then he thought to look again to see what it was that was caught there. **(365r)** It was a coracle, or skin-covered bag wrapped snugly all around. With his knife he cut it open and saw the forehead of a small creature. And when he saw it, he exclaimed, "Look at the radiant brow [*tal iesin*]." The creature in the coracle responded, "So let it be Taliesin!"

In the opinion of the people, this was the spirit of Gwion Bach, who had been in the womb of the witch Ceridwen, who gave birth to him and then cast him into the water or into the sea, where he remained in his coracle, floating in the sea from the early days of Arthur until the time of Maelgwn, which was about forty years. Now, this is far from sense and reason, but I will continue the story. It says that Elphin took the skin-covered bag home and handed it to his wife. She nurtured the spirit closely and dearly, and from that time Elphin's fortunes increased day after day, as well as his acceptance by the king.

Soon thereafter, the king was holding court in Deganwy Castle at Christmas, with all the **(365v)** lords of both spiritual and temporal worlds, as well as a multitude of knights and squires, who all spent their time praising the king: Is there in the whole world a king as rich as Maelgwn? And to whom has the Heavenly Father given as many spiritual gifts as God has given him—a face and form and gentility and might, as well as strength of soul? And with all these gifts the Father has given him, one gift that surpasses all the others, the face and form and bearing and wisdom and chastity of his queen. In her virtues she surpasses all the ladies and noblewomen in the entire realm. And in addition to all that they posed these questions: Whose men are braver? Whose horses swifter? Whose horses and hounds are more handsome and swift? Whose bards more knowledgeable and wiser than Maelgwn's? These last were held in high esteem among the nobles of the realm. At that time, no one could hold the office we now call herald unless he was not only learned in the service of kings and princes but knowledgeable in genealogies and arms and the deeds of kings and princes, as well as foreign realms, and the ancestors of this kingdom and especially the history of the nobility, and they all had to be quick with their answers in various **(366r)** languages, such as Latin, French, Welsh, and English. They also had to be excellent storytellers, possess a good memory, and have a firm command of poetry, to be ready to make a metrically correct englyn in each of the aforesaid languages. On this occasion there were twenty-four of these learned men in Maelgwn's court, the chief of whom was Henin Fardd.

When everyone had finished praising the king and his virtues, Elphin spoke as follows: "It is true that only another king can argue with a king, but if he weren't a king I would say that I have a wife who is as chaste as any lady in the realm. And I have a bard wiser and more knowledgeable than all the king's bards." Some of the king's friends told him about Elphin's boast. So the king ordered Elphin put in a strong prison until he could prove the chastity of his wife and the wisdom of his bard. Then he put Elphin in the castle tower with a heavy chain around his feet. Some say it was a silver chain because Elphin was akin to the king.

The story says that the king sent his son Rhun to test the chastity of Elphin's wife. The author says that Rhun was one of the lustiest, most wanton young men in the world and that **(366v)** neither woman nor maiden, however unblemished, could come away untarnished once Rhun had spent some time with her. As Rhun was hastening toward Elphin's estate intent on despoiling his wife, Taliesin told his mistress that the king had put his master in prison and that Rhun was coming to deprive her of her chastity. And so he had his mistress dress one of the kitchen maids in her clothes. This the noblewoman willingly and lavishly did, outfitting the maid's hands with the best rings she and her husband possessed. Taliesin then had his mistress place the young woman at the supper table. She now looked like his mistress, who in turn was made to look like the maid. And as they were sitting handsomely at supper in this guise, Rhun arrived at Elphin's home. He was welcomed warmly, for all the servants knew him well, and quickly brought to the chamber of their apparent mistress, who rose from her supper and greeted him warmly. Then she sat down again to her supper and Rhun with her. He began to tease and joke with her in lascivious language. The maid kept up her resemblance to the mistress, but the story goes on to say that she swooned and then fell asleep, for Rhun had put a **(367r)** powder in her drink. She slept so soundly, if the story can be believed, that she did not feel him cutting off her little finger, on which was Elphin's signet ring, which he had presented to his wife some time before. And in this way, Rhun had his way with the maid, and then he left with the finger and the ring around it as a sign for the king. He told him that he had despoiled her chastity and showed him the finger he had cut off without her waking up.

This news made the king very happy. He sent for his council and told them the whole story and then had Elphin brought from the prison to mock him for his boast. He said to Elphin, "You must know that it is nothing but foolishness for any man to trust in the chastity of his wife any further than he can see her. And so that you can be sure that your wife broke her marriage vows last evening, here is her finger as a sign to you, and your signet ring around it, after the one she laid with cut it from her hand as she slept. So you can't deny that she has lost her chastity."

To this, Elphin replied, "With Your Grace's permission, indeed I can in no way deny that that is my ring, because a number of people know it. But I firmly deny that the finger that this (367v) ring is on was ever on my wife's hand. There are three significant things, not one of which was ever on my wife's hands. The first, with Your Grace's permission, is that wherever my wife is now, whether sitting, standing, or lying down, this ring is too big for her thumb. But you can see clearly that it is easy to slide this ring over the knuckle of the smallest finger that was on the hand from which this finger was cut. The other thing is that my wife has never, as long as I have known her, let a Saturday pass without trimming her nails before retiring. And as you can see clearly, the nail on this finger has not been trimmed for a month. The third thing is that the hand from which this finger was cut was kneading rye dough within the last three days before it was cut off, and I assure Your Grace that my wife has never kneaded rye dough since she has been married to me." The story says that the king became very angry with Elphin for opposing him so vigorously in the matter of his wife's chastity, and he ordered him back to prison, saying he would not be released until he could prove his boast about the wisdom of his bard.

During this time, when they were together on Elphin's estate, Taliesin told (368r) his mistress that Elphin was in prison again because of them. But he told his mistress not to worry, that he was going to the court of Maelgwn to free his master. She asked him how he was going to free him. Taliesin replied in verses that said how he would come to the court, confront the king's bards, and best them all as they fell silent against his poetic onslaught. At the very end he had ready a curse upon Maelgwn for the wrong that he and Rhun had committed.

And then he took his leave from her and came to Maelgwn's court. The king was in his royal state, going to sit at dinner in his hall, as kings and princes were accustomed to do on high feast days at that time. Taliesin entered the hall and found a place to sit in an inconspicuous niche (368v) in an area where poets and minstrels had to pass on their way to do their duty to the king. It is still the custom in a royal court for them to proclaim the largesse of the king, except in these days it would be in French. And so the time came for the bards and heralds to proclaim the generosity and capability and strength of the king, and as they passed the spot where Taliesin sat, he stuck out his lip and made a blathering sound. The learned ones paid no attention to him but continued on until they stood before the king to do the customary courtesies to him. But when they opened their mouths to speak, they did nothing but blather senselessly. The king sat astonished and thought that perhaps they were drunk. He ordered one of the lords who were waiting on the table to go to them and ask them to come to their senses and remember where they were and what their duties were. This the lord did, but they did not stop their silliness, so he went to them a second and third time and asked them to leave the court. **(369r)** Finally, the king asked one of the squires to deliver a blow to the chief of them, who was called Henin Fardd. The squire took a dish and hit him on the head until he fell on to his backside. He got up on his knees and prayed His Grace to let him show him that their bad behavior was the result not of ignorance or drunkenness but of the potency of some spirit that was in the hall. "And," Henin continued, "Honorable King, you must know that it is not from a surfeit of drink that we stand here dumb, like drunkards, unable to speak, but because of the spirit that sits in yonder corner like a little creature."

The king ordered a squire to fetch him. The squire went to the corner where Taliesin was sitting and brought him before the king. The king asked him what sort of person he was and whence he had come. He answered the king in verse, saying, "I am Elphin's chief poet, and my native land is the land of the cherubim." Then the king asked him what his name was. He replied, "John the Divine called me Merlin, but now all kings call me Taliesin." Following that, Taliesin spoke of all the places he had been in this world and the next. All of this amazed the king, and Taliesin explained why he had come. . . .

(369v) After this, Taliesin sang a song to succor Elphin, whereupon a windstorm rose up until the king and his people thought the castle would fall upon them. So the king had Elphin released from prison immediately and stood him next to Taliesin, who then sang a song that caused the chains around Elphin to open. Now, this story is hard for anyone to believe. But I will continue. **(370r)** When Taliesin had freed his master from prison and verified the chastity of his mistress and silenced the bards so that not one of them dared say a word, he asked Elphin to make a wager with the king that he had a horse that was faster than any of the king's horses. This was done, and a day, time, and place was set, the place now called Morfa Rhianedd. The king and his people and twenty-four of his fastest horses were brought out. The course was set and the horses readied. Taliesin came with twenty-four rods of holly burned black. These he told the rider in charge of his master's horse to put in his belt, telling him to let the king's horses take the lead and, as he passed them, one after the other, to take one of the rods and strike each horse on its crupper and then let the rod fall to the ground and do the same to the other horses as he passed them. He told the rider to note carefully where his horse stopped. Taliesin led his master to that spot after his horse had won the race. There he had Elphin set men to dig a hole, and after they had dug to a certain depth they found a huge caldron full of gold. Taliesin said to Elphin, "You see here payment and reward for taking me out of the coracle and raising me from that time on." In that place there is a lake now, called from that time to today the Caldron's Hole.

AN UNFORTUNATE WITCH

NLW MS 5276Dii

Alfred was the king of Wessex from 871 to 886. Here again Elis displays his willingness to pass along a story remarkable for its account of magic and devilish spirits yet contrasts it with tales from Holy Scripture and says that the present one is not to be believed.

(531v) In the time of King Alfred, as the author William de Relegibus says, there was a witch in the town of Barkley at dinner among her neighbors. Suddenly, a young crow that she had nurtured for some time appeared and flew onto her arm. The bird cawed two or three times while looking into her face more intently than it ever had before when cawing. This stunned the witch so (532r) much that she let her knife fall from her hand to the floor. Her color changed, and she sighed heavily as she said, "Aha, behold the last day of my life in this world and the first day of the passing of my soul to its eternal fury." And with those words a man came to the front of the house and in front of all the people called the woman by name and said that her son and all her family had died suddenly in that hour at her home. The woman urged one among the group in the house to go quickly to the monastery in the town and get a young boy and girl who had recently taken up the religious habit.

When the abbot and the nun came before the woman and asked her what had happened, she told them, "I am on the point and in the situation where I am about to be with every sort of person who would practice the kind of wicked life and ungodly craft and art to which my soul is doomed. My hope has been, from the day I dressed you in religious garments until now, that my soul and my body might be saved through your paters and devotions, praying and beseeching for me day and night. At this moment I see clearly that your labor has been in vain. But I am asking you to take my body the moment I have died and bind it tightly in the hide of a deer. Then put it in a stone chest, cover it thoroughly with a layer of lead, put iron bars around the chest, and bind it with iron chains. After that is done, I pray you to take some of the monks and sisters with you to keep a vigil over it for three nights, singing and reciting as many as forty holy and godly psalms and various other holy prayers to intercede for my wickedness. And on each of the three days, have forty masses and other prayers said. And if you are able to keep my body from the host of demons for three days and three nights, you can then bury my corpse among the bodies of Christians in the cemetery."

(532v) And the story says that they arranged her body exactly as we have recounted, and it was brought to the church, where they kept vigil over the body just as she had requested until about midnight of the third night. At that moment, all the people present saw a huge man with a hideous face burst open the door of the church and then, standing over the body, ask it to rise up. The sound of the man's voice caused the people in the church to shiver in fright. The corpse answered and said, "I cannot rise, because of the weight of all the bindings that are upon me." To this the shadowy spirit answered, saying, "I will set you free, but with a bit of pain." Thereupon the lead, the iron, and the stone all shattered, and the spirit took her in his hand, brought her out through the temple door, and put her on the back of a black horse that was standing outside the door of the church. In this manner he led away her body, which was heard crying out as far as four miles away.

Here you have heard a strange and true story. Whoever may be familiar with stories from Holy Scripture which are true cannot believe that stories like this are true, any more than such dreams can be true.

THE RING AND THE NECROMANCER

NLW MS 5276Dii

This is one of the stranger narratives on the theme of necromancy, and one of the stranger ends for a practitioner of that art.

(540v) About that time, 1056, when Stephen IX became the pope, William de Relegibus writes that there was a great wedding in Rome between a nobleman of the realm and a maiden called Egiena. The story relates at some length that after the dinner the man took the wedding ring from the finger of the maiden he had married and put it on his own finger. After joking and playing with his bride and the ring around his finger, he went to play tennis. The ring hurt his finger as he hit the ball, so he took it off his finger and put it on the finger of a statue that was next to him. When he had stopped playing, he went to retrieve the ring from the statue, but, as the **(541r)** *Polychronicon* says, it had closed its fist on the ring. Astonished that he could not open the fist, he went to his supper, having carefully closed the door of the tennis room lest someone should go in there before he could return. As soon as he finished his supper, he took some of his trusted friends, to whom he told the entire story, and returned with them to the tennis room. They found the statue with its hand fully opened and with no ring on its fingers. This astonished him greatly, but as there was no remedy for the situation, he returned home. When the time came, he went to bed with his spouse. After the people had left the room, in between the two of them he heard or sensed a kind of dark something lying there, and it spoke these words to him: "Lucian, why are you not turning your love more toward me in this hour than to the morning, all of this hour, for you married me, the goddess Venus."

And because of these words, he and his wife became more fearful than before, so that they lay sleepless throughout the night. The next morning, Lucian secretly told all this to his father. The elder Lucian told this to the priest Palumbus, who, as the story relates, was the greatest necromancer at that time. After long discussion, Palumbus gave a letter to Lucian, telling him this: "Lucian, you yourself must go at a certain time of night and stand at the crossroads outside the city, where you will see some people walking behind a horse-drawn bier. And very carefully look to see who the last person is, deliver this letter to him, and listen carefully to what you hear." Lucian accomplished all of this. At that time, as the story says, he heard words saying, "O God, highest in heaven, when will the priest Palumbus come to an end for his falsehoods?" Following this, Lucian returned to the statue of Venus, on whose finger he found the ring, **(541v)** which, after tugging at it for a while, he pulled from her finger. Then he told all of this to the priest Palumbus, who told him to go home to his wife. This he did, and with her lived his life in joy while he was in this world. Shortly after this, the necromancer experienced such remorse that he cut his limbs from his body, and in this way he died.

TWO WOMEN AND A DEAD HUSBAND

NLW MS 5276Dii

Otto III was the son of Otto II and emperor of the Holy Roman Empire from 996 to 1002.

(490r) The author of the *Polychronicon* says that Otto III, the emperor of Saxony from 996 to 1002, had a very lustful wife. She often tried to get a lowly countryman to commit adultery with her. He **(490v)** always refused her. Finally, she told him that if he would not fulfill her desires the next time, she would have the emperor cut off his head. And so a short while later she sent for the man. Meanwhile, the man privately told the whole matter to his wife, who questioned and listened to him, and then he went to the empress. When he refused her again, she charged him with treason and being a traitor to the emperor for not doing her will. And so the emperor had the man's head cut off.

The wife put her husband's head in her apron and came before the emperor, who was sitting in the chair of justice. She addressed him this way: "Greetings, Honorable Emperor. I beseech the Heavenly Father to send you the grace to fulfill the vow that you are sworn to uphold and to keep—namely, to maintain the law, with just judgments for both weak and strong, widowed women and orphans, without prejudice and to preserve justice for the weak, destitute, and feebleminded." And having said that, she took her husband's head out of her apron and held it between her hands in front of the emperor's face and said, "O Emperor, I beseech Your Honor to tell me now what the person who had my husband's head cut off illegally deserves for that deed." The emperor said that the person deserved to have his head cut off in the same way. At that the wife said, "Aha, Lord, in fact you are the man." The emperor said, "How can you prove this accusation to be true?" "Through God's miracles," she replied, "and the verdict of fire and white-hot iron."

The emperor had all of this brought before his council, where, in the presence of himself and a large gathering, she walked through the fire and over the white-hot iron barefoot and unharmed. This stunned the emperor and his council. They set themselves praying to God for ten days without stopping. Then they returned to the council chamber to deliberate and examine the matter. But they were unable to decide the issue. So they immersed themselves in prayers to **(491r)** God to send them true knowledge of the matter. They persevered in this for eight days, and then again twice afterward, for seven days and for six nights. Within that time, God gave the emperor the knowledge that his wife, the empress, had immorally desired the man and he had not consented to her desires. And so the emperor punished the empress by consigning her to flames. Then, in compensation for the loss of her husband and the harsh judgment he himself had given, he gave the wife four castles and with them a bountiful estate, all of which lay within the bishopric of Bremen. And their names represent the number of days the emperor and councilors were praying for enlightenment, as just recounted: ten days, eight days, seven days, and six nights.

A SORCERER WHO FARED LESS WELL

NLW MS 5276Dii

It seems unlikely that there was a chapel in Rome called Caerselem. What matters is that the Welsh *caer-* is a loan translation of *jeru-*, and so the Welsh have the last word here. The papal succession is also confused: John XVII succeeded Sylvester II; Elis hasn't worked it out clearly.

(494r) At the time of Otto III, the emperor of the Holy Roman Empire, there was a great sorcerer named Sylvester in the country of France. Through the means of his magic he won the affection of the king of France, who eventually made him the bishop of Raymis. There he worked his magic night and day until he won the love of the emperor, who made him the bishop of Ravenna. From there he worked his devilish arts night and day until he was made the pope or bishop of Rome, succeeding John XVII, the bishop of Plesans, as Sylvester II. He was seated in the year of Christ 1097. The writing says that shortly afterward he asked the devil to allow him to keep the primacy for as long as he lived. The devil replied, saying, "You will be in that position or you will say mass in Jerusalem before your soul departs your body." With this answer the pope felt certain in his heart that he was assured of a long life in this world, because for certain he was not planning to go on a pilgrimage to Jerusalem in the land of Judaea unless he tired of this world. But his clever intention was of no avail, for a short time later he happened to say mass in a chapel in Rome called Caerselem. Immediately, he was struck with such illness that he was certain in his heart that he must depart this world. And so, as some of the authors say, he felt such compunction for his evil life that he had the town butcher cut off his hands and feet and throw them outside the city among the carcasses of the city's animals. Then he had his body bound to the tails of wild animals and then set free outside Caerselem, letting the animals drag him away wherever God saw fit, and he enjoined his friends to bury his **(494v)** body wherever the animals stopped. The story says they ran wildly through the city until they came to the temple of Saint John Lateran, where the animals stood meekly and quietly like tame animals. And so his body was buried in that place. And scholars hold that because of that his soul was saved.

[A later and smaller hand added:]

But authors say that he did a great deal of harm among the faithful.

HENRY II: PIGGYBACK FOLLIES AND AN UGLY PRIEST

NLW MS 5276Dii

Henry II was the head of the Holy Roman Empire from 1004 to 1024.

(519v) There is a good deal in writing about Henry II, the emperor of the Holy Roman Empire, who succeeded Otto III. Some of the authors say that he expelled all the bards or minstrels from his court, commanding that the money he would ordinarily give to the poets and minstrels on high feast days be divided among the mendicants who gathered outside the door of the court. William de Relegibus says that Henry had a sister whom he loved dearly, so much so that he would not allow her to go outside his court, for he wanted her to take vows and become a nun. The story goes on to say that Emperor Henry perceived amorous dallying between his sister and one of the court's scholars, which he noticed constantly day and night. And then, as the writing **(520r)** says, he happened to look out the window of his chamber one snowy morning in the direction of his sister's chamber. He saw her coming through her door with the scholar on her back, and in that way she carried him through the snow and deposited him in his own room, lest anyone see his footprints coming through the snow. Then she returned to her own room. The emperor kept this to himself, and a little while later he made the scholar a bishop and told him, "I order you on pain of your life that you do not ride horseback ever again, from this day forward, on woman or maiden." At the same time, he made his sister the abbess of a religious house and told her, "My sister, I command you on pain of death to refrain from ever carrying a scholar on your back from this day on." And when they realized that the emperor had seen their lecherous behavior, they mended their lives.

The same story says he was journeying through a forest in a part of Almania on the Sunday called Quinquagesima, the last Sunday before Lent, when he heard bells ringing, summoning people to mass at a chapel that stood beside the road. The emperor dismounted and entered the chapel. The *Polychronicon* says that what he saw was the ugliest and most grotesque priest anyone had ever seen, coming out to say mass. The emperor knelt, attending to the mass. But the story says that he was unable to pray to God, his mind preoccupied in thinking and marveling within himself about why God, the source of all beauty and splendor, would allow someone as repugnant, ugly, and foul as that priest to come so close to Him and to experience Him in majestic ceremony. The emperor continued to think this way until the priest sang or chanted this verse: "Scitote que dominus est deus," which means "Know that the Lord is God." The **(520v)** priest looked at the emperor very sharply as he said these words from the same verse: "ipse fecit nos et non ipse nos," which means "he made us and not we ourselves." The words troubled the emperor's heart, certain as he was that the priest was so holy that he knew what the emperor had been thinking. Because of that experience, the emperor made the priest a bishop soon afterward.

THE PROPHESIED DEATH OF EDWARD I (THE CONFESSOR)

NLW MS 5276Dii

Edward the Confessor was the son of Aethelred the Unready. He ruled the Kingdom of England from 1042 to 1066. The conclusion to this story is enigmatic, to say the least.

(532v) Some books say that King Edward received knowledge and warning that none of his line would possess the crown of the realm of England for a long time after him, as a punishment for the laxity of the men of the church and the rulers of the realm in serving the rule of God properly. God would give the crown and the rule of the kingdom to a foreign power.

The story also says that some pilgrims from this country were going to the Holy Land in the time of King Edward. It goes on to say that they encountered an itinerant preacher in the clothing of a white monk, who, after having a long conversation with them, asked them from what land and kingdom they had come. The story then says that the monk asked the pilgrims to (533r) greet King Edward when they returned. And as a sign he gave them a gold ring, a token for the king for the sake of God and John the Evangelist and the union between Westminster Temple and his court. He told them to deliver to him the gold ring that he held out to them. The pilgrims asked the monk who he was and what he was called so that they could tell His Grace the King when they returned to England who it was that greeted them and sent this sign to him. The monk replied as follows: "Let you understand that he will change his life on the tenth day after you place this ring in his hand. And from that time he will come to dwell in the land where I live and where there is joy without sadness and light without dark. And my name is John the Evangelist, and my dwelling is among the blessed with the Father, the Son, and the Holy Ghost." And after these words the monk suddenly vanished from them.

After that the pilgrims continued on their journey toward this island. But the story says that a kind of sleep fell upon the pilgrims within two or three hours after the monk departed from them or vanished. The sleep was such that they were unable to rise from it. As a result, they had to go off the main road and lie on the ground and sleep. After they slept for a while, they woke and stood up. After they looked at the land around them, each of them thought in his heart that it was not the same country or land where they had put their heads down to sleep. And so they crossed themselves, looking long at one another. And then one of them said to another, "Indeed, I think in my heart that this is not the land and country where we put our heads down to sleep, because when we put our heads down to rest we were not more than a day's journey (533v) from Jerusalem, but by my reckoning we are now in the country of England in our native land." And then, by asking help from the Heavenly Father, they walked on and finally met some people, whom they asked what country they were walking in. The people answered that they were in Caer Gangen, at the moment in the country of Locrinus. From there they went to Caer Ludd, and in the end they traveled hard until they came before the king. They told him about their travel from beginning to end in detail and about the meeting with the apostle. They handed him the ring as a sign of the meeting, which the king acknowledged. He took it gladly, giving praise to the Heavenly Father and to the holy apostle for sending him such knowledge of his death. After this, he gave an order to certain of his attendants to welcome the pilgrims, make a big fire, and keep them in the court until he could send for them again. Shortly afterward, he fell ill. According to the story, that was a little before Christmas Day. The story says that he rose for matins on Christmas Day but fell so ill that he had to go to his chamber before the service was half over. On Saint Stephen's Day he fell ill again, and on the feast of Saint John he was sicker still because he had attended the service. Soon after this, he had the aforementioned pilgrims sent for. He ordered them to tell all the people who were there in the king's chamber how they experienced the miracles of God and John the Evangelist in a journey of three days to Jerusalem and back to this kingdom in five days and five nights.

When the pilgrims had told the whole story, just as we have related, the king took the ring and passed it to the abbot of Westminster, who gave it to be kept carefully among the best (534r) of the relics of the temple. It was kept there in honor from that time until just before the death of Henry VII, when it was lost or vanished suddenly from among the other relics without any of the keepers knowing how. After this, the king fell into a swoon or trance, which he remained in for some time. As soon as he awakened and was in his right mind and could speak, they asked him what was happening with him. He had certain of his council summoned near to him, to whom he told how two men of the cloth from Normandy whom he had known before came to him. These men, so the story recounts at length, told him that none of his family would be king until a time when a green tree was cut down and one of its branches was cut from the trunk and planted a second time on the trunk or the root within three days. As soon as Eadsige, the archbishop of Kent, heard his words, he said that the king was babbling and out of his mind. The author of the *Polychronicon* says that it was not long before the townspeople found out about the king's condition. The king weakened day by day until the feast of the Epiphany. On that day he died, and that was on the fifth of January in the year of the age of Christ 1065, after having ruled this land for as long as twenty-three years, seven months, and three days. Some of the authors have written that his body was buried in Westminster Abbey in the same grave where his queen Godhwa [Edith] was buried some time before. The writing says that those present at his burial heard some words or a voice saying these words: "Next to this one, maiden." And another voice or phrase answering with these words: "Why did you betray yourself, (534v) this I never did."

SWEARING ON BREAD IN THE TIME OF KING EDWARD THE CONFESSOR

NLW MS 5276Dii

The second half of this story is a condemnation of men of the cloth for their careless behavior. Their response is to do as they have to do and nothing more—as the saying goes, "When in Rome . . ." Hence Elis's final comment.

(528r) About this time, as some of the books say, one Easter Monday King Edward was sitting at dinner in Lambeth, and the lords assisting at table were talking about the death of Alfred or Alrud, the king's brother. The conversation deeply annoyed Earl Goodwin, who was there present. The king, upset at what he saw and heard among the lords, shot a fierce look at the earl. The earl responded by holding up a piece of bread in his hand and swearing as follows: "I pray and beseech the Heavenly Father that this piece of bread go neither up nor down if

I were either the one or in agreement with others involved in his death." And then he put the piece of bread into his mouth and chewed it. Thereupon he lost his ability to speak and went from one swoon to another, unable to speak until the third day, when he died.

There was much talk and discussion among the courtiers about his death. Some insisted that it was the piece of bread that killed him, a miracle of God to show that he was guilty of that act and to show the punishment for a false oath. Others, his friends, said that it was paralysis of speech on the occasion that killed him, with which the author Marianus Scotus agrees. Yet some of the other books say that it was in the fourth year of the reign of King Edward that this happened. **(528v)** But it doesn't matter, because all the books record the same story.

The book also says that Sven son of Goodwin, who had married Judith daughter of Baldwin, Earl of Flanders, was away from the realm in Jerusalem, as we have shown earlier. He died near a town called Lycia. Also at that time there were certain devout men rebuking churchmen for their negligence by reminding them of the lives of the church fathers of various periods and times in the past. Most of the churchmen responded to the criticism very defensively, arguing that in the same way that people throughout the world protect their persons with various cloths as the nature of the weather requires, and just as it is proper for every sort of person to conduct himself according to the way and manner of the people among whom he moves, to wit, in the winter he must have various heavy clothing and in summer he has to wear light, thin clothes to protect his body from too much heat. And when he comes among people who are suffering and sick it is not proper for him to sport and be gay. Nor is it proper for a man who may be among happy and pleasant people to be sad and melancholy. And in the same way in the old days, the old, holy, wise, simple men who were bishops ruled the church according to customs and practices to which the remainder of the churchmen had to adjust their customs, practices, and dress.

And so it is among the leaders in every age from that time to this, a time of thought and custom, when the church has become frivolous and unsubstantial. It is exactly the result of this sort of thinking that mocking answers like this are used to excuse their faults and their shoddy governance.

THE REIGN OF WILLIAM II AND HIS DEATH

NLW MS 3054Di

William II was a son of William the Conqueror and was the king of England from 1087 to 1100. He was known as William Rufus in Latin and in Welsh as William Coch, both nicknames meaning "red." Floods, conversations with devils, and astronomical fireworks seem to be part of bad weather in this account, and all of them reflections on the people's evil ways. No less evil is the massive destruction of homes and religious institutions to create the royal Windsor Park, a crime against the values whose upholding Elis elsewhere in these accounts insists is the responsibility of rightful sovereignty.

Bad Weather

(15v) In the fourth year of William II's reign there was a terrible tempest, with thunder and lightning and a wind that blew the roofs off a church in Chep and the bell tower of a church called Bow Church. The tempest destroyed more than five hundred churches and religious houses within Caer Ludd and made great devastation in the church of Saint Paul in London, the monastery of Saint Swithin in Caerwynt, the abbey in Salisbury, and various other churches in other places in the realm. Indeed, the stories say that this tempest destroyed and burned as many as seven hundred churches **(16r)** and religious houses in many different places within the realm, in addition to private dwellings. . . .

More Bad Weather

(17v) During this time, as various stories recount, different people in various places in the **(18r)** realm claimed that they had conversations with devils on numerous occasions and times. At about the same time, wonders occurred in different places within the realm. Some of them were in the firmament, in tempests wherein the sea sent such immeasurable flooding as had never before been seen. Such a punishing downpour of rain fell from the sky that rivers flooded the surrounding lands. The *English Chronicle* records that in this time, floodwaters the color of blood flowed from a mountain beside the town called Hempstead in Berkshire and continued to flow like that for fifteen days and fifteen nights, so that the entire region could witness it. This water flooded some private dwellings that were in its path.

And in the tenth year of his reign, a comet or hairy star appeared in the firmament ten nights in a row around the feast of All Saints. The astronomers wrote various opinions, saying that the people were tending more and more toward evil ways and that the death of the king was nigh. The story says that the king and his father had as many as twenty-five towns and eighty churches and religious houses knocked down to make and enlarge a new park, which was thirty miles long and twenty wide. He destroyed many parishes to make Windsor Park. He brought in stags and other wild animals to be cared for. He took more pride and pleasure in them than in any of his possessions, and because of that all the nobles and commoners of the realm grew weary of his selfishness and neglect of them. Some people called him the Pasture King; others called him Shepherd of the Wild Animals. Some of the officials in his court advised him to cease his arrogance and his aloofness toward the commoners. As for the men of the church, he scorned them all.

The Dream and the End

(18v) Some of the books say that three monks from the same monastery came to the king's court. Two of them came to offer money to the king to be appointed abbot, for the abbot of the house had died a short time before this. The third monk came there only to see the king. But anyway, the story says that the three monks came as one before the king, who called each of the two monks who were presenting themselves, to talk to him. After he talked with each of them privately in the absence of the others and knew what each of them was offering, the king, grasping and greedy for money, called the third monk to him. He asked the monk what he would give to be appointed abbot. The story says that the monk eventually told the king that he would give the court nothing but the chance to see His Grace and to observe the foolishness of his brothers who were putting themselves in danger and peril by trying to buy an office and so being in greater pain and danger than ever before. And after this conversation and several others that would be too long to discuss here, the king gave the abbacy to the third monk. Indeed, the author says that the king never turned down money in his life except this one time.

The story about him also says that King William Rufus or Red William saw this strange dream shortly before his death: He was in his bed asleep when he saw a doctor approaching him with a lancet in his hand, letting blood from one of the veins in his body. From the vein a stream of blood shot toward the sky until the firmament was dark from the amount of his blood. And **(19r)** the story says that from the horror of the dream he awoke terrified. Seeking answers, he told the dream to some of his council, who gave him the best advice and solace they could come up with. Nevertheless, they were afraid of saying something too negative to him too soon. But still neither he nor his council could see how he could avoid the fate that was against him.

The next night after this, the story says that one of the monks from the monastery at Westminster had a strange dream, in which he thought and imagined that he saw King William Rufus approaching the monastery bold and proud, and a large number of men both before and behind him, which seemed to him to be despising and scorning the king greatly. In this way he saw the king go and stand before the main altar, from which he saw the king take the image from a cross in his hand in a disrespectful manner and put it into his mouth, and it seemed to the monk that he bruised the image with his teeth. And irreverently, like a man in a rage, he took the image from the cross and threw it to the ground so that it broke into tiny pieces, all of which he shamefully crushed under his feet. At that moment, the monk saw a column of terrible flame shoot from the head of the image to the roof of the temple. The monk awoke frightened from the vision and told it to the abbot and some of the monks, who marveled at him long afterward. Then, as the story goes on, the monk told the vision to a knight named Sir Hammond, who was close to the king, and urged him to tell it to the king and advise him to be careful with himself, because the monk had secretly told the knight that he understood through this dream that there was some dire threat to the king. The knight told all of this to the king and to some of his council. They advised the king to do penance for his sins and ask God for mercy and forgiveness and to turn to ways as God saw best, desiring and entreating the king to be wary of his chamber and his court for some time until such a thing as signified by the dream failed to happen and passed by in some other form, for some of them believed that the dreams meant bodily harm. But nevertheless, he laughed at them.

(19v) The morning after the king had broken his fast, he took some of his knights to hunt with him in the new park. There, as my author has recounted, the king happened to see one of the stags kept to shoot at with a long bow, which a knight called Sir Watter Turell did. I don't know whether the king told him to shoot or whether he did that on his own. But it doesn't matter, as the writing says that the knight shot toward the animal immediately. The arrow struck a branch of a tree above the animal's head and glanced off, striking the king in his breast. He died from that wound, and because of his promiscuity he did not leave a legal heir to succeed to the crown. He died on the first day of August, having been the king of England for twelve years, one month, and twelve days. He was buried in Westminster in the year of the age of Christ 1100.

THE DREAM OF HENRY I AND MATILDA

NLW MS 3054Di

Henry I, who ruled England from 1100 to 1135, was a son of William the Conqueror and Matilda of Flanders. He married Matilda of Scotland. His daughter Matilda was also known as Maude.

(26v) King Henry I decreed, with the consent of the Lords and Commons of Parliament, that the empress Maude, his daughter, was the heir apparent and the true inheritor of the crown and (27r) ruler of the realm of England after him. And to confirm this action, the king had allegiance and fealty sworn to the empress by having David, the king of Scotland, and William, the archbishop of Kent, and many of the princes of the realm swear an oath on the Bible and on relics that they would stand with the empress in the right of the realm against anyone who might provoke dissension and disunity against her and her heirs if he happened to die without leaving male heirs.

Around this time, as the story goes, the king had a strange dream. In his sleep he saw a great number of scholars in harness rising against him. They were fully armed, cruel and angry and threatening to kill him. And behind the scholars, he saw a host of bishops in harness rising up against him and threatening to kill him. And after these, he saw a troop of knights rising up in harness and threatening to kill him, just like the others. In fear and terror from this dream, the king deeply repented his misdeeds. After this he did right by many of the scholars, bishops, and men of the church whom he had wronged by releasing to the knights and laymen of the realms the tribute of the geld. And to please God, in a manner of speaking, he made a religious house in Caer Gaint, which he filled with the Grey Friars, and these were the first of the order of Saint Francis ever to come to this country. About the same time, he had the monastery at Reading built and refurbished the monasteries at Merton and Cwmhir and various other religious houses and churches in addition to these.

In the twenty-eighth year of his reign, there was a betrothal and marriage between his daughter Maude, the empress, and Geoffrey Plantagenet, Earl of Anjou. Between them they had a son who was called Henry. The authors say that Henry I built Windsor Castle, Bristol Castle, and Berkeley Castle and a religious house of the Grey Friars, which he had built in Normandy. In the thirtieth year of his reign, as the author Ranulf writes, Robert, Earl of Flanders, (27v) died, and the author says that Flanders then fell to the king of England as the true heir because he was next in blood because of his mother. But the author does not say that the title is incorrect. After the marriage of the empress to this aforementioned earl, the king dwelt in Normandy, where he ingested a surfeit of eel, as some of the books say, but other books say that it was an injury resulting from a fall from a horse that caused the wound and injury, but it really doesn't matter which of the two caused his injury, because all the authors agree that he became ill with a serious sickness about the time when a son was born to the empress. The son was named Henry, after his grandfather. Soon after this, the king died in Normandy without male issue from his body, having borne royal and kingly honor over the English realm for thirty-five years, four months, and eleven days. His body was brought across the sea to this realm, and thence from Gower. The passion they felt for him caused the death of some of the men who were guarding his body. He was buried in the monastery of Reading in the year of the age of Christ 1135.

After his death there arose numerous songs of praise of him by various poets, songs that spread from the tongues and hands of musicians throughout the world. And it's safe to say that the proverb is true, the one that says "Whosoever desires praise and fame, let him go from his land or let him die." And indeed, in his time not very many people could give him a good word, but after he died many of them praised him mightily. But still others of his people would not fail to speak openly of his sins and how his body was while he lived on earth, sunk in three of the seven deadly sins: lust, cruelty, and adultery.

THE EARL OF ANJOU WHO MARRIED A SHE-DEVIL

NLW MS 3054Di

This narrative begins with reference to Geoffrey Plantagenet, though it is really about his father, whose reputation is considerably tarnished in the story. Geoffrey was said to be handsome, and Henry I was so taken with him that he arranged a marriage between his daughter Matilda (also called Maude, or Mallt in Welsh) and Geoffrey. Their son married Eleanor (Elinor) of Aquitaine and became Henry II of England.

(52r) Some of the writers of France and Gaul say that Geoffrey Plantagenet was the son of one of the earls of Anjou. That earl married a she-devil because of her looks and appearance, and according to the story he had four children by her before he knew she was a she-devil, although many people had been pointing out various signs to him that showed she was not a human. One of the signs they pointed out to him was that he could in no way get her to stay in the church when the priest was saying mass. The story goes on to say at length that the earl perceived that she would not stay in the church when the priest reached the canon of the mass, at which time she would vanish suddenly. And so, according to the *Polychronicon,* the earl ordered four of his knights to watch over her and her four children, who accompanied her every day, two on each side of her, one in front and one behind and one on each side of her in the church. There, as the *Polychronicon* says, the knights stood around her, one in front of her and one behind and one on each side of her. They were to be watchful of her and take hold of her cloak. But still and nevertheless, as soon as the priest began to read the canon of the mass, she suddenly flew from their grasp through the roof of the church, and with her the two children who were on her left side. All the people of the congregation saw this, but no one ever again saw anything of her or of the two children she took with her.

One of the two children who remained or whom she left behind her was Geoffrey Plantagenet, Earl of Anjou, who married the empress Mallt and was the father of Henry II of England. The story says that this Geoffrey was so wanton and promiscuous that he had an affair with **(52v)** Elinor daughter of the Earl of Poitou when she was the queen of France. Because of that the king of France divorced her, as some of the writings say. But even so, all of the authors agree that this Elinor married his son Henry. And her father, as the author of the *Polychronicon* says, was so wanton that he raped one of the wives of his most distinguished aides, whom he married while her husband was still living. That caused a learned man of his country to satirize him for that act, but the earl took it as a joke. And so, as the story says, the man, who was devout, beseeched God that he should never have a graceful and noble descendant from his line. And as the author of the *English Chronicle* writes, that is why Henry son of Geoffrey, Earl of Anjou, is so graceless and ignoble.

EDWARD III AND THE GARTER

NLW MS 3054Di

Edward III, the son of Edward II, ruled England from 1327 to 1377. This charming if fanciful story tells of the founding of England's highest order of knights and its motto, "Honi soit qui mal y pense."

(165v) King Edward III held a splendid feast for the nobility of the realm at Windsor Castle, where, as the story says, he was born. And this feast, if the books can be believed, was begun at the beginning of January in the nineteenth year of his reign. Edward Baylol, the king of Scotland, **(166r)** came to the feast, and Edward, Prince of Wales, and as many as nine earls and a great number of knights and countless squires and leading men of the realm and many foreigners from various nations and realms and lands far and near. And if one can trust the writing, people from far away as Turkey came here.

For the occasion, the king decreed the pride of place to the honorable Order of the Garter, as the highest order of knights within the realm, just as the Knights of the Golden Fleece were the highest of the Holy Roman emperor and the Knights of the Order of Michael were the highest grade of knight under the king of France. Before this time, there were not in this realm but two grades of knights, one that was made in battlefields and the other of the sort that were ignored, the Knights of the Carpet. And there had been the Knights of the Round

Table, the order that had been held in high esteem among the ancients long before. In their place, as some of the books opine, Edward III proclaimed the Order of the Knights of the Garter, on which these words were written in French: "Honi Soeit qui mal pens." This means in Welsh "Gwarth i'r neb a feddylia drwg," "Shame for the one who thinks evil."

According to the story and popular belief, these words had been said some time earlier, to protect the integrity and reputation of a lady of his court whose garter came free and fell from her leg to the floor as she was dancing one day with the king. He saw the garter, bent down, and picked it up and handed it to the lady. Some people who were watching them saw this and were taken aback. This upset the king, and so he spoke the words quoted above. Some people hold the opinion that it was from love of the lady that he had these words put on the garters of the knights of the order. But some others insist that it was King Richard I, or Richard Heart of a Lion, who started this order while giving siege and assault to the Turks at the city of **(166v)** Acre. There, in the heat of battle, only twenty-six knights remained among his force. He gave each of them a patch of blue leather to place as a thong around their legs so that he could recognize them in that livery when he next encountered them. Long afterward, these were called the Knights of the Blue Garter.

But really, it doesn't matter who it was who started this order, because all the books say clearly that at that time this order was considered the noblest among the nobles in this part of Europe. And the words quoted above are used today of the knights who wear this garter—to wit, "Shame on those who think evil!"

THE PLAGUE IN THE TIME OF EDWARD III

NLW MS 3054Di

Edward III survived the plague and ruled for another twenty-seven years afterward. The number of teeth in the jaws of his thirteen children is unknown.

(174r) About this time, in the twenty-third year of the reign of Edward III, the people of the realm became full of pride and arrogance and every other evil, and so the Heavenly Father sent a scourge to punish them. He sent a great death of Black Plague and pestilence in the eastern part of the world, in Turkey and Sardinia, and from there it went to Italy, and in the process this plague depopulated that part of the world so that there was but a tenth of the people living on the earth in those countries after the plague as there had been before it began. And around the end of the same year there fell such an assault of water from the sky, especially in England, where, if one can believe the written accounts, there was not twenty-four hours of dry weather at any time without rain either morning or night from Christmas Day to the feast of John the Baptist in summer. And this moisture or wetness grew like a disease in people and animals to the extent that people died quickly in this realm in such numbers that the living were not able to bury the **(174v)** bodies of the dead, one after the other wherever they fell, as well as a lack of space and time to bury them and lack of land to bury them in. And so they made a wide and deep trench, in which they placed one layer of bodies and then placed another layer of bodies and soil over that. They worked like that day and night until the hole or ditch was full of bodies up to the edge. The story says that more than a hundred bodies went into each ditch before it was closed up tightly over them. And still the story says there was a lack of consecrated land in which to bury the dead in numerous towns and cities of England and especially in Caer Ludd.

The story says that at that time as many as sixty-four thousand bodies were buried in the cemetery of the Charterhouse, which is on the north side of the city next to Saint John's Hospital, and that was after having filled all the churches and cemeteries of all the church parishes and religious houses of the city and the several cemeteries within the city that had been consecrated and so could serve at the time.

And in this time of death there were marriages without ardent affection, and there was scarcity and want and fleeing from place to place without relief, because the story relates that people of the realm fled and ran away from one place to another to escape Death, to whom God had pointed out his victims wherever they might be. The account also relates that the children who were born after this plague did not have as many teeth as had been in the heads of their forebears in past times by as many as four teeth—namely, two in each jaw. The story goes on to say that there had been as many as forty-four teeth in the mouths or in the jaws of their ancestors, but since that plague there are but thirty-two teeth—that is, sixteen in each jaw.

HENRY VI AND HIS GLOVES

NLW MS 3054Dii

Henry VI was the king of England from 1422 to 1461 and again from 1470 to 1471 after being deposed by Edward IV. He was the son of Henry V and Catherine de Valois.

(333v) A short while after King Edward IV calmed the disquiet in the realm, King Henry VI died, a prisoner in the white tower. But of what or how he died there have been many stories and plenty of strange opinions among the people of the realm from that day to the present. Some of the people said that King Edward sent various men at various times to the prison in the tower to assassinate or to kill King Henry. But as soon as these men would come to the king's chamber, not one of them could in their hearts do any harm to his body. The text says that he often said to the men who came to kill him as follows: "Indeed, not one of you can in your hearts do any harm to me, and there is no man born naturally from the womb of a woman who can in his heart kill me." And certainly, in the opinion of the people he was a saintly and religious person, and it was said that he often went from his captivity in the tower to a church in the town of Barking, which was west of the tower, and at other times to the chapel of Saint Carne, which is east of the tower. And to prove that he did this, he left his gloves one day before the image of Mary in the chapel at Barking. One day as he sat at his meal, he asked one of his keepers to ask permission of the lieutenant to go to that chapel to look for his gloves. They were, he said, one on top of the other, and the fingers of the top glove were standing straight up. The lieutenant thought this a (334r) strange story, but nevertheless he sent some of his trusted men to the chapel, where the gloves were found just as the king had said. They were shown to the lieutenant, who took some of the men of King Edward's council and went to King Henry's chamber. They questioned him closely, trying to find out how his gloves got there. He told the lieutenant, "Well, I go diligently two or three times a week to one of the two chapels that you keep for me as long as my soul is in my body."

Now I must turn to the people and their opinions. Some believe that he was suffocated shortly after the events discussed above. Others said that his death was the result of a conversation between King Edward and his brother Richard, Duke of Clarence. The duke told the king that he was amazed that he had allowed King Henry to live as long in this world, given the stories that were going around about him among the people of the realm and the disquiet and disturbance that he had caused so often in the past within the realm. It is said that King Edward replied to his brother, saying, "Aha, Sir Richard, truly I have wanted in my heart to be relieved by his having been dead and buried. And yes, I have shared my intention many times with some of my closest men, who went there determined to kill him, but when they got to him none of them were able to do him any harm."

Not long after this conversation, the Duke of Clarence took some of his men and went to the tower and to the chamber where King Henry was being held. If the opinion of the people can be believed, the king welcomed the duke warmly, saying, "Yes, yes, your hands would do the deed that many another intended to do to me ever since I came to this prison." And with those words, Richard of Gloucester pulled out a dagger and stabbed the king in his chest. The king died on the spot.

Here one could scoff at this story and ask why he had not been born naturally from his mother's womb just as other men have been and are born. Indeed, the people believe clearly that his mother did not deliver him as she did her other children—rather, she was pregnant and (334v) carried him in her womb for more than a year and a half, at which time they had to cut open her womb to bring him out of her. It is said that at that time he had long teeth, which is unnatural. This agrees with the story that this work has told, that King Henry had not been born naturally from a woman's womb, so that no man was able in his heart to kill him.

But it doesn't matter at all how King Henry was killed, because all the books agree that he died not from a sickness. His body was buried in a monastery in Saint George's chapel, which lies along the river Thames between the town of Kingston and Windsor, the commemoration of this burial taking place in the summer around the feast of Corpus Christi. Soon the more foolish people of the realm would come there on pilgrimage, believing that he was a holy, saintly martyr. But despite that, I have seen and heard many of the old people who had seen him and knew him, who say that they did not believe there was any of that saintliness or holiness in him.

THE DEATH OF EDWARD IV

NLW MS 3054Dii

Edward IV was the great-great-grandson of Edward III. He succeeded Henry VI and ruled from 1461 to 1470 and again, after Henry's brief second reign, from 1471 to 1483. Elis's claim here that he was in the eighteenth year of his reign when the plague struck cannot be true. The word that Elis uses is *deunawed* for *deunawfed*, "eighteenth," but perhaps he meant *nawfed*, "ninth," which works here. But the rest of the chronology is also problematic, except for the year of his death, which was 1483.

(336v) In the eighteenth year of the reign of Edward IV there was much death in London from the Black Death or plague and also in most of the realm. It continued from one place to the next throughout the land for as long as five years, up to the beginning of the twenty-third year of Edward's reign. Then, as some of the books show, the king fell ill from the disease, as some books and (337r) people believe. But other books and other people say firmly that the king died before he fell victim to the disease, for both writings and opinion hold that the king was fat and stout and had big feet. It is said that his feet were fourteen inches long and the queen's feet were twelve inches long. The queen had to lift her gown when she walked in the court, a practice that was soon followed by noblewomen throughout the realm. It is also said that the king was gluttonous and bigmouthed, to the extent that one day, as the king was riding across London Bridge among his nobles, a woman of the town asked a friend which of them was the king. She was told that the king was fair, elegant, of proper bearing, "but really he has one of the biggest mouths I have ever seen on a man." The king heard those words, turned his horse's head, and said, "True, fair woman, I have a large mouth, but indeed my mouth is not so big that I can't do twice as much about another mouth!" These words embarrassed the woman deeply. And in the same way, the writings show that he was fickle and capricious, so that it was difficult for anyone to count on his promises or trust his word. He was also one of the lustiest men in the realm.

Around that time, if one can trust a few people or some of the books or the talk of the old people, it was in London that he got a mortal wound in the city from a merchant who had a handsome wife.

To have his way and his desire with her, the king, accompanied by two or three of his closest men, came suddenly to the merchant's house, where he intended to have his way with the wife, even in front of her husband. But the writing says that the man came out from a corner where he had been hiding and with a dagger stabbed the king in his side. From that wound the king died a short while later.

There is some doubt about this, because some say that it was in London that he died from this wound, but others say that he was taken wounded from London to Westminster, where all of the books agree that he died, but they don't agree about the cause of death. He died on the ninth day of the month in the year of the age of our lord Jesus Christ 1483, having had royal rule over the kingdom in war and peace for as much as twenty-two years, one month, and eight days. His body was buried in Windsor. He left behind three children, a son named Edward and three daughters, who were married in England.

LLYWELYN, PRINCE OF WALES, AND THE FOOL

NLW MS 3054Di

King John, the son of Henry II, ruled England from 1199 to 1216. Llywelyn ap Iorwerth is known in Wales as Llywelyn Fawr, Llywelyn the Great. He was the king of Gwynedd and eventually ruled practically all of Wales. He was killed in December 1240. Llanrhychwyn is a small village near Trefriw, an area closely connected with Llywelyn Fawr.

(90r) After the death of Iorwerth Drwyndwn son of Owain, his son, Llywelyn, took the chaplet of the prince of Wales. In the fifth year of the reign of King John, there was a betrothal and marriage between Llywelyn, or Lord Llywelyn, and Elsabeth [Isabella], the second daughter of King John, as some of the English chronicles say, but the Welsh chronicle says that he married Sioned, the youngest of the three daughters. But indeed, it doesn't matter which of the two, because all the books say clearly that he married one of the daughters of King John and that the prince made great preparations to go to England for the wedding. The story says that the prince's fool begged and pleaded earnestly with his master to be allowed to go on this journey with the prince, but his **(90v)** master refused the fool's plea, and a short while later Lord Llywelyn took to horse and made his way from Maenan to

Rhuddlan. On the second day, he journeyed from there to Caerleon on Dyfrdwy, where, as some of the Welsh books say, the prince encountered the spirit and shape and manner of his fool, whom he had left behind and who had followed him from there to Caerleon. The prince ordered the innkeeper to hold the fool there securely until he could get someone to take him back to Trefriw. Then the prince rode on until he came near to the court of the king. Then and there, the fool suddenly appeared in sight of the prince and his retinue. The story goes on to describe how the prince had the fool dressed in frivolous and humble clothing of the sort that typified a person of little intelligence.

Lord Llywelyn came to the court, where, in due course, he married the king's daughter. My copy says that at the wedding feast there was no lack or shortage of every sort and variety of excellent and rare specialties to set before the humble and rustic Welsh. They passed the time in pleasure with every sort of entertainment, with music and song and magicians and sorcerers. These last were much in demand at that time in the courts of kings and princes. One of the king's enchanters came forth to display his art to entertain the people at the feast. To mock the ignorant Welsh, he produced, through the magic of his art, two or three men dressed like the Welsh, driving a herd of goats through the hall or chamber where the wedding was taking place. As soon as they came into the hall or chamber, they began bounding about on the hearths, the benches, and the tables, running from place to place through the people, who were laughing and shouting, "Look at this, a gift from Wales!" The spectacle appalled the prince, making his blood rise to his cheeks from shame and embarrassment, and he asked the magician why the goats signified the Welsh rather than other, lower peoples. The magician replied, saying, "Because (91r) they're ready to run and jump from one place to another all across this realm and across the sea to other lands and other kingdoms to make mischief as goats do." And at those words the prince bowed his head without saying a word.

Thereupon the prince's fool stood before his master and asked permission to demonstrate some of his magic before the gathering. "Well," replied the prince, "I have enough to be embarrassed about without giving you permission to give me more reason to feel shame." Nevertheless, the story says that eventually, through the fool's persistence and the support of others, the prince gave the fool permission to do what he thought appropriate to do. My copy shows that with his magic, the fool had some men drive a herd of pigs into the hall or chamber in the same way that the king's magician drove the goats there. As soon as the pigs came into the hall or chamber, they began to root up the floor and overturn the tables and trestles and do various other piggish actions which would be too long to recount here. The Welsh all laughed at this, saying, "Here you see a fine gift of English pigs to the prince to root up ferns for Llanrhychwyn." This stunned the English, who asked the fool why the pigs were there. He replied, saying that they represented the English peoples, whom he said were pigs estranged from their faith and rooting up the land like pigs to make fields and ditches of the country's earth and land to keep it for a small number of them, all of whom are more alien to one another than dogs are to pigs. This greatly cheered the heart of the prince, who not long after took his leave of the king and journeyed toward Wales. He made good progress until he reached as far as the dark thicket above Llaneurgain, where the fool appeared before the prince.

(91v) "Sir, it was in this place that we encountered each other, and it is here that I will leave you. Be assured and certain that I am not a part of nor related to your fool, whom you suppose that I am, the one you have in your court when you are at home, which he never left." And at that, he suddenly vanished from their sight. The prince continued on his journey to Trefriw, where he found his fool, who had never left the place. This seemed a great mystery to the prince and his people.

RICHARD I, THE LION, AND THE HEART

NLW MS 3054Di

Richard I was the son of Henry II and Eleanor of Aquitaine. He ruled England from 1189 to 1199. He is known as Richard the Lionhearted or Richard Coeur de Lion.

(73v) King Richard prepared to return from the Crusade to his kingdom, and so he put the governance of things into the hands of the captains whom he had left behind and whom he intended to leave in charge of the towns and castles that he and the Christians had won in the lands in that part of the world. He sent his queen in a ship and a small group of people with her from the port of Jaffa to the port of Lystra, where he intended to meet her. He made his way toward that place by land with a small group of people and finally arrived at Lystra to meet the queen. There some men set upon him, intending to take him prisoner. He escaped from there to Aquileia, near Venice, a land and realm that belonged to the Duke of Austria. He traveled along the land quietly and stealthily with a few people on his journey until he came to the town of Friesach, ruled by a man named Friedrich, who aimed to seize him and imprison him. But he escaped from there, leaving some of his people behind. Hastily, he rode from there secretly toward Germany. But the duke sent his messengers with an order to the Earl of Limbach, commanding him to seize the king and his men. They did so near the town of Memmingen and from there sent him to the Duke of Austria. The duke kept him in a narrow cell for a month. After that he sent him as a prisoner to the emperor Henry V, who kept him in a narrow cell from then until the next Saturday of the Flowers.

Some of the books say that the emperor then had him taken from his cell and brought before him and his council to answer to charges that had been brought against him. On that occasion, as some of the books relate, King Richard gave such compelling responses that the emperor's ire was abated and he praised the king and gave him great honor.

And yet the English books tell us about him in some detail at that time and say that he **(79r)** had sexual intercourse with the emperor's daughter and that he killed the emperor's son. Because of all of this, one can believe the stories that say the emperor had the king put in a strong tower beside the place where he kept gluttonous lions. The emperor ordered that one of these beasts be kept hungry for a day or two and then released suddenly into the king's quarters to kill him. The king got word of this plan from the emperor's daughter, according to the story. She gave him a towel of fine linen and told him to wind it tightly around his arm and wrist and hand along with a sharp knife, which she told him to keep in his hand. All of this he did as she advised, and as soon as they let the hungry lion into the tower or chamber of the king, it attacked him with its mouth wide open. The king, like a bold and fearless man, thrust his hand and arm down the lion's throat with the knife in his hand and plunged it into the lion's heart, which he then cut out of its body. Word of this came to the emperor, who immediately had the king brought before him. The writings show that the king brought the heart with him in one of his hands, and if those writings can be believed, he ate it with some salt in the presence of the emperor. Because of that, as the English account says, he was called Richard Heart of the Lion.

However, the German stories say that it was because of his boldness and bravery in the successful siege of Acre that he was given this name. And I am not able to find in any reliable work that he did any of these things, either ravish the emperor's daughter or kill his son or kill the lion, as the English books say. And for that matter, it is likely that these accounts are but flattery and praise from the English poets, just as every generation of Britons has said of King Arthur. And I have certainly never seen any real authority for why the Duke of Austria and the emperor Henry V seized and imprisoned King Richard, as a number of authors have claimed, though they give no reasons for that.

OWAIN TUDUR AND CATHERINE DE VALOIS AND THE RISE OF THE TUDORS

NLW MS 3054Dii

Catherine de Valois was the wife of Henry V and mother of Henry VI. In this story, Catherine uses a disguise to trap Owain Tudur. This brings to mind the way in which Elphin's wife uses disguises to foil Rhun's plans in "The Epiphany of Taliesin." In the tales of the births of Hercules and Arthur, Jupiter and Uthyr employ magic and shape-shifting to achieve their respective unions with Alcmene and Eigr (see parts 1 and 2). It would seem that women can achieve their goals with wile, while men require magic. There is now a folio missing after folio 307v; fortunately, Professor Jerry Hunter copied this story from the manuscript years ago, before it disappeared.

(305v) According to some of the accounts in the English books and the opinion of the English people, the council of England would not allow Queen Catherine, the widow of Henry V, to marry anyone in England. She was full of desire and longing, for she had been widowed for some time. At the time, one of her servants, her server at meals, was a squire from Gwynedd in Wales. He loved one of the queen's handmaids, and the queen perceived this.

One day in summer, beside the queen's court, this squire was swimming in the river that flowed beside the court. The handmaid saw him there and quickly told the queen about it. **(306r)** The queen went to the window to look at the men swimming. Among them she noticed one of the men, who surpassed his mates in the fairness of his flesh. She asked her handmaid who the fair-skinned man who was in the water with the others was. She replied that it was the Welshman Owain, her server. "Aha," said the queen, "you see there the man who loves you very much." "That's so," said the noblewoman, "that's what he says. Indeed, I can't go anywhere out of your sight where he is not trying to pursue me." "Well," said the queen, "let me go as you in the evening to a place where you are likely to meet, and I will see to it that he will not force himself on you ever again."

Some time later, the handmaid set a time to meet Owain in a gallery beside the queen's chamber. The handmaid then told the queen about the meeting between her and Owain. The queen dressed in the handmaid's clothes and in the dark went to the gallery where Owain was awaiting his love. He put his arm around the queen's neck, intending to kiss her on the mouth, but she turned her cheek to his mouth. After they had exchanged a few words, he noticed a light as if the queen had returned to her chamber, so he tried to give her a kiss on her lips as he was leaving, but once again she turned her cheek. This made him think that she was not his love, so he bruised her cheek with his teeth so that he could discover who was mocking him in this way. And then the two of them parted to get out of the light. The queen went to her chamber and Owain to his lodging.

On the following day, the queen ordered her chamberlain to ensure that Owain would be her server at breakfast that day, and so he did. After Owain had arranged her food on the table in the order required by his office, he turned his face toward the queen, who had been washing to prepare for her meal. She cast a fierce look at Owain as she put her finger to her cheek, where he (307v) could see the plaster covering her bruise. His face fell as he realized in his heart that it was the queen whose cheek he had bruised on the preceding night. Because of that, according to the opinion of some of the books, he intended to take to horse and ride back to his country, for fear of the queen. However, she, according to some of the people, sent a messenger after him, who found him in his lodging pulling on his leggings and preparing for his journey to Wales. The messenger ordered Owain to return to the queen. According to some other people, the queen had sent orders to the porters to keep Owain within the court. But it doesn't matter by which of the two means he was returned to face the queen. What matters is that within a short time she was so taken with him that she was set on marrying him.

According to the opinion of the people, she sent one of her heralds to Wales to find out his ancestry. The herald went to the house of Owain's mother, where she was sitting by the fire, eating her meal from her knees and her lap. The herald asked about Owain's lineage, which she gave to him in writing. The herald returned to the queen, for whom he embellished the encounter, as men of their profession are bound to do, telling the queen how he found Owain's mother sitting by the fire on her estate, eating her dinner from two tables, the worse of which he would not sell for a hundred marks, and he repeated to her Owain's lineage from the father's side and the mother's.

Not long afterward, the queen secretly married Owain. Soon after that, she became pregnant by him. That amazed the king's council, who queried her about it. In some detail, she told them that it was her married husband, Owain, who had made her pregnant. And so the council seized Owain and imprisoned him.

Even so, he had two sons by her, Edmund and Jasper. Thanks to the efforts of their mother, the two were made earls. Edmund was proclaimed Earl of Richmond and Jasper Earl of Pembroke. And that was in the third year of the reign of Henry VI, until the fourteenth year of his reign, when he made his brothers earls. Not long after that, Owain's head was cut off in his prison for marrying the queen, who died a short time later.

HENRY VII AND NECROMANCY

NLW MS 3054Dii

Henry VII, known in Wales as Harri Tudur, was the first king of the House of Tudor; he ruled from 1485 to 1509. He was a grandson of Owain Tudur, who married Catherine de Valois: one of their sons was Edmund Tudor, the father of Henry VII.

(349v) After King Henry VII returned to England from France, he set his mind and his goal on accumulating money and on keeping the realm in peace and tranquillity so that he could accumulate wealth under his control. He knew well what it was to be poor and penniless, in the grip of which he had been leading his life for so long, as well as being in great peril and fear for his life. Through these experiences, he acquired sense and wisdom, so he knew what sensible and wise leaders could accomplish with worldly wealth. He saw that with sufficient treasure under his control he could easily rule faithful princes as he saw best. And indeed, our ancestors used to say that he was the wisest and had the best sense and the best goals and intentions of all the kings who ruled from the Conquest up to his own time. According to the opinions and stories of some of the old people, he was skilled and learned in the arts of astronomy and necromancy and had a deep understanding of the meaning of prophecies. He delved deeply into all of the books of prophecy in Wales. Many of the men in England believed that no one in the country could plot any sort of harm to his body that he did not know about, despite the secrecy with which they had planned it. They supposed that it was certainly through the study of the aforementioned arts **(350r)** that he got such knowledge. However, other people believed firmly that it was the barefoot friars, the Franciscans, who made him learned and wise. They had won a place in the hearts of the people by that time. Both nobles and commoners told their secrets to them when they found the time and the place, either through confession or in some other way, for they believed that these friars were the saintliest men in the world. The king and his council held them in high regard. Indeed, the king was so taken with them that he had a religious house built beside his court in Greenwich for them, men who had been living in shacks made of gorse and grass along the Thames River beside the court at Greenwich since the time of Edward I. To these and their community of false priests, nobles and commoners alike were bringing their confessions.

THOMAS MORE AND THE GARDEN OF PAIN

NLW MS 3054Dii

Sir Thomas More, canonized in the Catholic Church as Saint Thomas More, is a controversial figure, to say the least. He is well known throughout Christendom for his polemical writings against such Reformation figures as Martin Luther, William Tyndale, and John Calvin, whom he considered to be heretics. He eventually became one himself, in a sense, in that he refused to recognize Henry VIII as the head of the church in England. This text supports the argument that he was ruthless in his attacks on heretics. See the following story for more.

(494r) At this time, Sir Thomas More, the chancellor of the realm, was taking great pains in questioning thieves and such men as he held to be disloyal. He had built a new mansion on the shore of the Thames, above the monastery of Westminster, where a house and barn of his had burned, along with one or two other barns of his neighbors (he had been meeting in chamber, of which this work has treated earlier). It happened in a remarkable way, like this: As his servants were leading his oxen home from the field, an axle on one of the carts caught fire, and flames shot out from the hub. The flames reached the stalks of corn, which ignited a fire on the carts being unloaded within the barn. This started a firestorm in the corn and stalks and the buildings, **(494v)** so that no one was able to save them without getting burned. Many people were amazed at the accident, and at the time everyone had an opinion as to the cause. Some said that a few people from the town of Chelsea secretly placed fireballs that would explode inside the barns, out of jealousy and anger toward More for buying and then driving them out of their houses and halls and lands as he had done. Some of those men were owners of lands within that town and cultivating land in the field that lies between the aforementioned town and the town called Kentstown. Others said that God sent that vengeance upon him as a punishment on him for ruining his neighbors. And indeed, he no longer took interest in agriculture from that time, nor did I hear that he made amends to those men he had wronged.

At the time, he was making a wall of mud and straw around a kind of orchard and garden, within which he brought the kind of soil that the aforementioned barns had been standing on. Within this garden there were a variety of trees and places to sit beneath their branches. The trees had various names, such as Tree of Suffering, Tree of Conscience, Tree of Punishment, Tree of Confession, Tree of Truth, Tree of Joy, and Tree of Release. At each of these trees, one after another, he would interrogate such men as he held either because of a person accusing them of being a thief or for having committed a felony and against whom people had made complaint in various places in the country. According to the stories of people who lived with him at that time, he would inflict great suffering on the men as he questioned them about the several matters that people had accused them of doing, until they confessed to the deeds of which they were accused. First he would inflict suffering upon them under the tree named Suffering. He would put iron presses on the fingers of both hands of such people, and the presses were tightened on their fingers until blood could be seen flowing from the base of their nails. Around the heads of others he would put a cord in which many knots had been tied, and the cord was then tightened and pressed **(495r)** around the head until the aforementioned knots cut into the skin and the bone. With other men, he had their feet placed in a pair of hot boots. Still others he tortured with different sufferings, the kinds of torments that would be too long to detail in this work. When he felt that he had reached them through such cruelty, he led them under the Tree of Truth, where he let some of them live by confessing to the sort of deed that none of them had ever dreamed of committing. But for many a man, it is better to suffer death than suffer a minute of this kind of torture again. In that way, he took pride and pleasure in the torture of such people. And this was a great wonder for a man of great learning and great intelligence, as he was taken to be, to do.

SIR THOMAS MORE AND THE NECROMANCER

NLW MS 3054Dii

The latter part of this tale seems to reflect the controversy between Martin Luther and William Tyndale on one side and Thomas More on the other. In his fight against heretics, More also opposed Henry VIII's separation from the Church of Rome and the annulment of Henry's marriage to Catherine of Aragon. Henry's response to More's opposition was to behead him. John Frith was martyred in 1533 for his liberal views on religious tolerance.

(496r) In May of 1530, in the twenty-fifth year of the reign of Henry VIII, Lord Thomas More was deprived of his position as lord chamberlain. His office had been in the hands of the Dukes of Norfolk and Suffolk for a while, but then a lawyer named Master Audley became the lord of the seal of London. But I have never heard why the king and his council dismissed Sir Thomas More, though everyone has his opinion about it. Some say that he asked the king and his council permission to give up his office. At that time, a man of his acquaintance asked him why he wanted to give up his office. He replied that he would then have more time to write against the heretics. Others say that the king found fault with him for accusing a scholar who was subordinate to him, a scholar called Master Reich. Because of that he was deprived of his position. But while he was still in office, he wrote a great book which he called a confutation or defeat of William Tyndale and his followers. A short time after that, Sir Thomas More made over his entire estate to his wife and his children, his houses, his mansions, his land, property, and wealth. All of that he gave into the possession of his wife and children. This astonished many people. Many thought that he was so learned that he had knowledge of how he would die, but others said that it was through necromancy. And indeed, it was alleged that he kept someone of that art with him for some time. The person was finally exiled and went to Calais, where he practiced his art to induce people to flock to him. Because of that, the deputy of Calais ordered him to leave the country. He did leave Calais but then went to the nearby town of Marck, where men and women from Calais and the countryside followed him to seek knowledge from him about things unknown. Other came to him to ask about goods that had been stolen from them. **(496v)** Still others came seeking information about what their wives would do, whether they would be faithful to them or not, and in the same way the women wanted to know if their husbands would remain faithful to them.

At the time, a merchant from Calais encountered a man named John Frith on the road from Calais to Marck. Because there was an old friendship between the two, the merchant invited the scholar to turn around and come with him to Marck to have a meal. He told the scholar what it was that made him go there at that time. The scholar was much aggrieved about that matter, saying that he thought it a great wonder for a faithful Christian to give any credence at all to such an ungodly art as that, an art and practice so obviously against the laws of God. But despite that, the merchant took such pains with his response that the scholar decided to come with him to the town. Along the way, the scholar said to the merchant, "Well, Simon, you are making me accompany you on this journey against my will, but I say to you in God's truth before we get there that the man will not be able to do anything while I am in his sight."

After a while, they arrived at the town of Marck, where a number of honest men from Calais were having a meal with this scholar or person who seemed to be an assistant to Simon Jennings and was seated at the lowest end of the table. After the meal, this magician or necromancer brought out his crystal mirror at the head of the table. He set a certain young man to look into the mirror and then to the priest to conjure the spirit, which was a long time in appearing. The priest asked the boy what he saw in the mirror. The boy replied that he saw the shadow of a man sitting in a chair with a pen and ink in his one hand and paper in the other. And after a few words of magic, he ordered the spirit to show the boy true information in writing about whatever he was asked. After some words, the writing in the glass showed that he would not write information about anything earthly at that time except in either Hebrew or Greek. The priest then looked around and said that as there was no one present who could understand either of those two languages, there was no point in pursuing the matter further at that time. But one man **(497r)** who was at the table said, "Let him show information in the one of the two languages he sees best." It happened that there were one or two present who could understand it. After these words, he asked the spirit to write that information in the language he thought was proper. Then the boy read the writing, which was as follows: "I will not reveal the information at all as long as the man who is wearing religious clothing and is sitting at the lower end of the table remains in the house." Because of that, the priest said several angry words to Frith, asking him to get up and leave the house. Frith replied that people of faith ought to drive him and his devilish practices out of the house and out of the world with a horrible death.

After dinner the Calais men turned toward home. The next day the necromancer left and was never more seen near Calais.

A GHOST STORY FOR HENRY VIII

NLW MS 3054Dii

Henry VIII was the son of Henry VII. He ruled England from 1509 to 1547, a period when Elis was busy compiling his chronicle.

(567v) The king [Henry VIII] observed the Christmas holidays at Hampton Court because there had been numerous deaths in London in the preceding autumn and beginning of winter. But there was much talk in private from one ear to the next, both in court and around London, that it was because of certain unrest and rumor that there was a spirit within York Palace near Charing Cross. It was said that there was a spirit in the place causing much disquiet. According to the people, it gave out a great scream like a raving killer, which horrified all who heard it—not only the ferocity of the voice but the noise and clamor of the windows and the doors in the place opening and shutting. The first scream would open the doors and windows, and the next scream would shut them. At the time, it was said that a strange man had come to the mayor of London and had told him many weird tales concerning the king's body. The mayor sent the man to the king, where the man relayed the strange things, which included the creature that inhabited York Palace and various other things that I will not recount here. But whatever tales the man told to the king or whatever the reason, it is certain that the king did not spend any time within the walls of the court by Charing Cross from the beginning of July to the first of March in the following year.

RHOBIN DDU

NLW MS 3054Dii

Rhobin Ddu flourished around the middle of the fifteenth century. He wrote many prophetic poems and elegies, one on the death of Owain Tudur.

(324r) About the time of the death of Edmund, Earl of Richmond, in 1456, there was a great prophet and poet in Gwynedd named Rhobin Ddu, master poet. If tales of the Welsh can be trusted, he was able to show things that were likely to happen long before they did happen. He told Sir William Gruffudd, who at that time was the chief chamberlain of Gwynedd, that the Earl of Richmond would wear the crown of the realm of England. Soon after the knight received proof of the Earl of Richmond's death, he sent for the poet, to whom he said in mocking words, "Aha, fair Rhobin, see how well your prophecies are working. You made me and many others believe that Richmond would wear the crown of the realm, as you told me many times. But now I see clearly that your babble is nothing but fraud and deceit." The poet, provoked and angry, replied, "Sirrah, though the Earl of Richmond has died, his body burned and his ashes buried, still his wife is pregnant with a male heir, and that man will be the king of England."

As a result, according to a story widespread among the Welsh, the chamberlain held the poet prisoner until he could get confirmation that the lady was pregnant. Afterward he freed Rhobin, who made his way south to Deheubarth. And if you can believe any part of these stories, he was in Pembroke Castle when the lady went into labor. On his advice, she took a room in the tower, where she gave birth to her son, who, as the old people of Wales say, was named Ywain at baptism. But when the bishop told the lady his name, she had him change it and name him **(324v)** Henry. Still, the men of Wales prefer to call him Ywain. When he had come of age, he fled the realm and went to France for fear of King Edward.

Much later, Rhobin visited the old chamberlain, who was building a palace in Caernarvonshire in a place called Penrhyn. As they conversed, the chamberlain asked Rhobin what he thought of the progress of the work. Rhobin replied that indeed the work was fine, "if you were able to finish it." "Why do you suppose I will be less able to finish it than I am now?" asked the knight. "Well," said Rhobin, "I can only tell you a true story. If the body of a one-handed and one-eyed woman in a blue petticoat floats along the Slatey River from Menai and comes to land beside this palace, it is safe to say that neither you nor your son will ever finish the palace." And not long after, such a body did come with the tide from Aber Menai to Aber Ogwen, and the chamberlain died soon afterward, leaving the palace unfinished, as it is today. And of these happenings and various others of these silly tales, it would be too long to treat in this work and at this time.

CHARLES V AND THE ASTRONOMER

NLW MS 5276Dii

Elis does not quote any of his usual sources for this story, so it is likely that it was current in oral tradition or perhaps just in the news when he was working on his chronicle. The tale is a familiar one, of course, of the Spanish exploration and exploitation of Mexico and the Aztec Empire.

(439r) When the emperor Charles V went to Spain in 1521, he was warmly received among both nobles and commoners. At that time there was a skilled astronomer who had gone to Spain. He had been in England, explaining to the king that there were certain lands and islands unknown to most of the world and that they were wealthier than almost all of Christendom. The astronomer asked the king to give him some ships, men, and provisions to travel to those lands and to conquer them and make them subject to the English crown. The king refused, and so the astronomer left England and journeyed to Spain, where he displayed his knowledge and skills to merchants and sailors. These men believed his story and promised to commit ships and provisions to journey and seek these lands and islands, which he claimed that no one in these parts of the world had ever visited or seen, if it would please the emperor to provide a captain and permission to recruit soldiers and sailors to accomplish the journey. The matter was laid before the emperor, who, having approved of the venture, agreed with the request of the merchants and gave them license from his court in the town of Valencia in Castile in August of the year of the age of Christ 1522. That was when the astronomer and his people took to their five ships.

The emperor sent a man named Hernán Cortés to serve as the captain and governor of the group in his place. When all was ready, they took to their ships and struggled for some time, until **(439v)** at last they caught sight of the land they were seeking, a land called, in the native language, Siocatán [Yucatán]. They landed at a harbor with a fine fortified town, which Hernán Cortés and his men conquered and which he named the City of the True Cross [Veracruz]. He built a strong tower there, in which he settled a number of Spaniards to keep the town under control while he and the men of his company traveled the land, to which he gave the name New Spain. He stayed in that area to teach the people obedience to him in the name of the emperor. Many people of that region came to complain to him against an unreasonable lord whom they called Montezuma. They said he dwelt in a city called Tenochtitlán, a domain that consisted of villages and fortified areas of everything that pertains to wealth and the sustenance of man and beast. All this Hernán would soon see for himself. The extent of this realm was as much as two hundred and twenty leagues, counting three English miles to a league, and in this area there were many fortified towns and villages. Within the realm, every owner of land was under obligation to Montezuma. Tenants were obliged to pay him duty from every town and city, and every village and territory would have to pay such fine things as varied from those things their neighbors paid. As a result, Montezuma was the epitome of wealth of every sort of thing that grew out of the earth and every sort of thing that was mined from the earth, such as gold, silver, and fine stones. The book says that Hernán told the emperor about the nature and layout of the country, indicating that the king could place more than four hundred thousand soldiers in that land. The book says that there were numerous fortified towns and as many as twenty thousand dwellings in such towns, built with hewn stone in the most splendid way you can imagine or have ever seen in Italy or any country throughout Christendom. The courts of the king were built with a variety of colored precious stones, such as marble, jasper, and alabaster. And if one can believe this account, the country has more wealth both within and without than all of Christendom, whence great treasures have been coming to the emperor every year from that time to today. The entire story of this land would be too long to tell in the present work, so I will treat of this matter no further.

GLOSSARY

The identity of persons and places is clear from the texts in many cases but in others not so clear.

Alba/Albania/Albion	old names for Britain in general and Scotland in particular
Alcmene	wife of Amphitryon
Aldan	mother of Merlin
Almania	homeland of the Alemanni, now a part of Germany
Aloth/Dianoth	kinsman of Uthyr Pendragon
Amon	ancient Egyptian god of the air and the sun
Amwythig	Welsh name for Shrewsbury
Baylol	Edward Balliol, king of Scotland
Bow Church	church on Bow Road, London
Bremensis	Bremen, northern Germany
Bwlen	Boulogne, France
caer	Welsh for "fort, stronghold, castle"
Caer Collwyn	"Hazelwood stronghold," name for Harddlech (English Harlech), according to Elis
Caer Cyffin	"Border [or frontier] stronghold," modern Aberconwy

Caer Deganwy	stronghold at Deganwy, a town near Llandudno, north Wales
Caer Digoll	"Flawless stronghold"
Caer Efrog	Welsh name for York
Caerfyrddin	Carmarthen, a town in south Wales
Caer Gaint	Canterbury
Caer Gangen	unknown; possibly from *cangen,* "branch"
Caer Goel	stronghold of Coel Hen, an early British king
Caer Haas	*see* Caerwys
Caerleon on Dyfrdwy	Caerllion on the Dee, English Chester
Caerllion ar Wysg	Caerleon-on-Usk, a town in southeast Wales bordering Newport
Caer Llwydcoed / Caer Lwydcoed	Lincolnshire
Caerloyw	Gloucester
Caer Ludd	Welsh name for London
Caerselem	normally "Caersalem," Welsh for Jerusalem
Caer Sidia	the Otherworld fortress, associated with Merlin and Taliesin
Caerwynt	Welsh name for Winchester
Caerwys / Caer Haas	town in Flintshire, site of an important eisteddfod (arts, music, and literature festival) in 1523
Capel Gwial	King Arthur's "Chapel of the scepter"
Caswalldan Lawhir	Caswalldan (or Caswallawn) "Long hand," the father of Maelgwn Gwynedd
Cerdicus	Anglo Saxon king of Wessex
Cerrigle	"Stone place," Stonehenge
Chaunceford	town in Essex
Chep	Chepstow
Childeric II	king of the Germans
Chwitsen	Welsh borrowing for Whitsun, Welsh Sulgwyn
clas	Welsh for a community of individuals in common cause
Colgrim	a leader of the Anglo-Saxons against the Britons

Custennin the Blessed	father of Emrys and Uthyr Pendragon
Cwmhir	Cistercian monastery near Llandrindod Wells in Wales
Cynnydd Gain Farfog	foster father of King Arthur
Dianoth/Aloth	kinsman of Uthyr Pendragon
Edeirnion	a region in Denbighshire, Wales
Eigr	Welsh for Igerna
Emrys	Welsh form of the Latin Ambrosius; son of Custennin and brother of Uthyr Pendragon
Engiest	Welsh spelling of Hengist
englyn	a strict-meter form of Welsh poetry
Galia	Latin for Gaul
Gawen	Gawain
Geoffrey of Monmouth	author of *Historia regum Britanniae*
Gildas son of Caw of Britain	author of *De excidio a conquestu Britanniae*
Glen Ebron	Welsh for Hebron
Glyn Galabes	unknown
Gorlois	husband of Eigr (Igerna)
Gwenddydd	sister of Merlin
Gwenhwyfar	Welsh form of Guinevere
Gwrthefyr	son of Gwrtheyrn (Vortigern); also called Vortimer or Vortiporius
Gwrtheyrn	Vortigern
Gwynedd	early kingdom of north Wales
Hafren	Welsh for the Severn River
Harddlech	"Beautiful rock," now Harlech
hippocras	wine flavored with sugar and spices
Jesses	possibly the Jutes
Lambeth	a borough of London, early site for the archbishops of Canterbury
Lancelot du Lac / Lancelot of the Lake	first knight of the Round Table
Llanelwy	Welsh for the town now called St. Asaph

Llaneurgain	Welsh for Northop, Wales
Llanrhychwyn	village near Trefriw, north Wales
Maelgwn Gwynedd	sixth-century king of Gwynedd in north Wales
Mordred	King Arthur's nephew
Morfryn Frych	putative father of Merlin and Gwenddydd
Myrddin	original Welsh name for Merlin
Nannerch	town in Flintshire, Wales
Nant Conwy	"Valley of the Conwy River," in northeast Wales
Octa and Offa	sons of Engiest (Hengist) and brothers of Rhonwen
Polychronicon	Latin chronicle by Ranulf Higden
Raymis	Rheims, France
Rhonwen	daughter of Engiest (Hengist) and sister of Octa and Offa
Rhun	son of Maelgwn Gwynedd
Rhuthun	town in Denbishshire, Wales
Rhydderch Hael	one of the progenitors of the ruling dynasties in sixth-century north Britain; also called Rhydderch Hen
Saul Benuchel	Saul "High chieftain," the father of Maelgwn Gwnedd's wife
Strond	Old English name for the Strand, a principal route in the city of London
Suthland	Welsh for Sutherland in Scotland
Thetford	ancient town in Norfolk, site of a Cluniac priory from 1104
Uthyr Pendragon	son of Custennin, brother of Emrys, father of King Arthur
Vortimer/Vortiporius	son of Vortigern (Gwrtheyrn); also called Gwrthefyr
William de Relegibus	for "William *De legibus*," William of Auvergne
Ynys Fon	"Isle of Môn," Welsh name of Anglesey island

Founded in 1893,
UNIVERSITY OF CALIFORNIA PRESS
publishes bold, progressive books and journals on topics in the arts, humanities, social sciences, and natural sciences—with a focus on social justice issues—that inspire thought and action among readers worldwide.

The UC PRESS FOUNDATION
raises funds to uphold the press's vital role as an independent, nonprofit publisher, and receives philanthropic support from a wide range of individuals and institutions—and from committed readers like you. To learn more, visit ucpress.edu/supportus.